BANTU

Bantu Boy

Growing up in Kenya

ROGER STOAKLEY

YOUCAXTON
PUBLICATIONS

ISBN 978-1-914424-68-7
Published by YouCaxton Publications 2023

YouCaxton Publications
www.youcaxton.co.uk

Roger Stoakley:
telegraphrs@gmail.com
tel. 01823 412580

To my Wife, who has patiently cared for many young people.

The characters in this book are entirely fictitious

by the same author:

My warriors and I

Kenya, land of contradiction

CHAPTER ONE

My name is Winstone Wamalwa. Of course, I don't remember the time when I was born, but the memory of what befell my family when I was three years old is etched in my mind and will remain so for the rest of my life.

I looked up from the table on which was laid a pencil drawing of two oxen pulling a cart. It was a delicate drawing, full of detail. The oxen looked so real it was almost as if you could touch them. My grandmother was leaning over me looking at the same picture. She was a tall, unsmiling and uncompromising woman and her drab brown headscarf and long cream dress liberally sprinkled with grey and brown flowers reflected her personality.

'That is a drawing made by your mother,' she commented.

'I know,' I replied. 'I pulled it out of a drawer in our house.' I contemplated the drawing for a moment then looking pleadingly at my grandmother. I asked the inevitable question. 'When shall I see Mama again?'

Grandmother sighed and shook her head. She was losing patience with me. Would I never accept that she had gone forever?

'You will never see her again. She's dead now you know, just as I have said before.'

Those words cut into me.

'Dead, dead, dead!' I screamed. The agony of losing my mother was more than I could bear. 'Dead, dead, dead!'

It couldn't be true. I scrambled from the table and ran outside to the old orange tree. Flinging my arms round the trunk I burst into tears and began banging my head against the bark. It was not the first time I had assuaged my anguish against that tree. There was still evidence on my forehead from previous outbursts. "Dead" was a word I dreaded. Even at my young age it spoke of finality; the end of the short, carefree life I had come to know. Now the home that had nurtured me lay empty, devoid of the parents who had provided the love and security so essential to the welfare of a young child. Grandmother looked after me, fed me, clothed me but rarely showed any love towards me except in my fits of anguish.

'Come my little one,' she said, prizing me from the tree. She carried me back and sat me down on her lap. 'Come Wanyonyi. Let me put my arm round you and stroke your forehead.'

It was her way of calming me down. It was on occasions like these she called me by the name my parents had given me - Wanyonyi - rather than my "Christian" name of Winstone. It was a requirement of the missionaries in Kenya that every child presented in church be given a Christian name. But as time went on, names were often chosen which related not to saints or characters from the Bible but to famous people from colonial times. My parents had chosen the name not realising it was the incorrect spelling of a once famous prime minister they had learnt about in school. And so Winstone it was and Winstone was the name by which my family and friends called me, whereas Wanyonyi was reserved only for the most intimate family occasions. The name first given to a child was often regarded as having a special significance relating to the moment of birth. Some claimed the name given at that time had a spiritual significance and as such should only ever be used by the closest of family members.

After a while I calmed down. The despair I felt at the loss of my mother subsided for the time being. Yet both I and my grandmother knew sooner or later it would arise again when something occurred to trigger the memory of her. Even now, the anguish I experienced throughout my childhood is such that I can hardly bear to think of it. Therefore, I have had to leave much of it to others who watched me grow up, to tell my story.

§

The small farm on which Winstone had spent the first years of his life was in a remote part of Kenya, close to the Ugandan border. It was an area of gently undulating land, a warren of footpaths and murram tracks, little fields, clumps of trees and rocky outcrops, the remains of ancient volcanic activity. And all was watched over by the brooding hulk of Mount Elgon which, in its benevolence, bestowed a multitude of little streams to water the fertile soil spread about its feet. It was a land largely overlooked in colonial times and even now the appearance of a white man was something of a wonder. It was a land where, in the past, wandering tribal groups had crossed and re-crossed and finally settled, each with their own culture, rituals, taboos and language. There was a time among Winstone's people before the advent of Europeans and their multifarious competing religions, when the people worshipped the universal God, Were Khakaba, creator of heaven and earth. At that time there was no religious conflict in the land and everyone looked to their one and only God for their strength and wellbeing when confronted by the vicissitudes of life. It was a time when everybody knew their place in society, a time of great kinship.

Delia, Winstone's mother, came from a family with money. She was her parent's favourite child and the eldest of several brothers and sisters. She grew up to be a beautiful and graceful girl. Not only was she good-looking; she was gifted as well. Her younger siblings had neither the abilities nor the comeliness with which she was endowed. They regarded her with admiration tinged with jealousy. Academically bright, she did well as a primary school pupil and spent her secondary education at a boarding school where her aunt lived. The aunt was friendly with a family from a village nearby and it was through her that Delia came to meet Jeremiah, the eldest son of a subsistence farmer. The family were poor, but Elias and Martha, Jeremiah's parents, had saved enough to send their children to school. Jeremiah had none of the attributes of Delia. He was a simple boy, thoughtful, honest, kind and loving. Delia was attracted to him at first sight. They fell in love and eventually married and Winstone was their first-born.

Delia's family was upset by the marriage. They had assumed she would continue to university, get a good job and help to support her less able younger brothers and sisters, but Delia was independent and a country girl at heart. The thought of going to university, living in a city and perhaps working in an urban environment thereafter was not what she wanted.

When Delia married into Jeremiah's family, she acquired four brothers-in-law and a sister-in-law.

John was the second born. He was a bright child, and after schooling obtained a good job in a government department in the town of Eldoret. John had married shortly after Jeremiah. He and Miriam his wife already had a daughter and a son, Petra and Michael, and Miriam was now carrying their third child. Crispin, John's next eldest brother was unmarried. He was a long-distance lorry driver living down on the coast. He loved his job and was always on the move, often driving from the coast as far inland as Kisumu on Lake Victoria or up to Moyale on the Ethiopian border. The family saw little of him except when he had some holiday. Then came Catherine, a kindly, practical and resourceful girl who was training to be a nurse, a profession for which she was much suited.

The two youngest boys were twins, Matthew and Mark, who worked on the farm. They were regarded as the black sheep of the family. They were quite unlike the rest of the children. From an early age they had run wild. They were unruly, indolent, disobedient and uncooperative. They not only offended their parents by their behaviour, they also offended the neighbours. When they were young, hardly a day went past when Elias didn't have to take out the cane to beat one or other of them for misbehaviour. When they were old enough to attend school, they caused mayhem in class, were caned by the teachers and frequently sent home. The twins were regarded as misfits by the community and not surprisingly had few friends. This upset Elias. He agonised over their behaviour. He was a pillar of the church, a kindly, caring man who spent much of his time helping others and was well respected in the community. Yet he felt tarnished by the behaviour of these two sons.

'One day,' he said to Martha, when he had been particularly irked by them, 'God will reap divine retribution. You see if it doesn't happen.'

In some ways he blamed himself for them being so different from their siblings. Martha was a loving wife. They had been sweethearts from an early age, had grown up in nearby villages and had been to school together but because they came from poor backgrounds their schooling had come to an abrupt halt for want of school fees. They therefore never finished their education. Had their schooling been completed, a better opportunity in life might have opened up for them since they were both very bright children. As it was, subsistence farming was the only occupation they could turn to.

When Martha was pregnant with the twins, Elias didn't take a second wife as so many of his neighbours had done, but instead he had a relationship for a while with another woman in the village. When Martha found out she was desperately angry and deeply upset. At the back of Elias's mind was always the thought that his indiscretion and the anger it caused his wife, might have affected the children she was carrying.

Matthew and Mark worked alongside Jeremiah and their father on the land but their input was half-hearted. Why should they exert themselves when in the longer term, after the death of their father, their older brother would manage the farm? It was Jeremiah who decided what crops they would plant. He was the planner, the organiser and did the larger share of the work. Keenly conscious he had both his parents and a family to feed and clothe and therefore needed to cultivate as much produce as he could to sell at market, he was an assiduous farmer. He would be out on the land while the dew was still on the grass and rarely finished work before sun-down whereas the twins were late risers and often took long breaks during the day. They were concerned only to ensure they had enough food for themselves and never gave a thought for the needs of their parents.

Delia was adored and trusted by her parents-in-law. They regarded her almost as a daughter. In return she loved their simple, honest, hardworking lives. When she married, she acquired a sewing machine and was skilled at making clothes for them. When Jeremiah's parents were ill, it was she who looked after them. When they had visitors, it was Delia who set about the catering and since Elias had little experience of handling money, she took responsibility for looking after the family finances.

It was not until five years after their marriage that Jeremiah and Delia were successful in producing a child and therefore, he was all the dearer to them. As a toddler he adored his father. When he was upset or in trouble he would invariably call out for Papa and strong arms would come to pick him up and cuddle him. Jeremiah was tall like his mother, well built with twinkling eyes under bushy eyebrows and a face with a ready smile. When he hugged Winstone and closely cradled him in his arms, the warmth of his father's body against his, Winstone felt comforted and safe from harm. The two became inseparable. As soon as he could walk, he followed his father everywhere. Whether he was tending the cattle or out working on the land, Winstone staggered after him, his bare feet treading warily over the warm earth, the stones and the hummocks of grass.

The twins used to laugh at Jeremiah when they saw Winstone trailing behind him and call out, 'Hi Jeremiah, there's that shadow following you.'

Jeremiah would grin and say, 'He's training hard to be a future farmer of this land.'

By the age of three Winstone was busy helping his father in the fields. He helped with weeding, learning which weeds to pull out in-between the rows of cabbage and sweet potatoes and then carefully shaking the soil off the roots before laying them aside to die in the sun as he had seen his father do. Some of the weeds were deep rooted and he had to pull them out with both hands. Sometimes the roots suddenly let go of their grip in the soil and Winstone would fall back on his bottom laughing and giggling as he picked himself up from the ground. At other times he fed the chickens, teasing them by clutching the grain in his hand and making them chase after him until he threw it down.

He loved the farm and he loved his home, and at three years old, he was at an age when his young mind was absorbing the sights and sounds of childhood that would remain with him for the rest of his life. There was the smell of new mown grass and of the earth as rain fell after a long dry period, of cow manure as it dried in the sun, the smell of wood smoke as it curled out of the kitchen door, the early morning dew on the grass, cool to his bare feet, the sound of water being drawn from the well, the clang of pots and pans being washed, heavy rain trampling on corrugated iron roofs, the crystal clear night sky studded with diamonds and the crow of the big white cockerel at first light as it announced the beginning of another day. Sometimes in the evening when he had finished working outside Jeremiah would reach for his *litungu,* and plucking the strings, begin singing softly to Winstone who sat on his Mama's lap learning the songs and clapping his hands in time with the music. These evenings were special for

Winstone. The world outside silenced by darkness and the little family of three huddled around the glow of a hurricane lamp created a cosy and intimate atmosphere which made him feel at ease and eventually sleepy and ready for bed.

Then one day his father was no longer there for him. He could not find him anywhere. He was not out in the fields, nor tending the cattle and not around the house. When he cried out, 'Papa, Papa,' there was no reply. In the house his mother sat weeping. At his young age he could not understand where Papa had gone and why Mama was crying. He himself had cried many times when he had fallen or got lost or had a fright, but he had never seen either parent cry. They had no need to. In his mind they were grown up and in control of things and so there was no need for them to be upset.

Suddenly he felt terribly alone. Where were the comforting arms and the smiling face? When he asked her where Papa was his mother didn't reply. Gone was the gentle, loving, smiling Mama he was used to, the one who always came and tucked him up in bed, sang songs to him and kissed him good night, leaving the sweet scent on his cheek that she often wore, a scent which comforted him and reminded him of her until he fell asleep. Now she looked pale and withdrawn and hardly noticed him when he put his hand on her knee. He didn't understand why he couldn't find Papa. Papa and Mama always enjoyed each other's company for they were very much in love. Where was Papa now and why didn't he come to her when she needed him?

He crawled up onto her lap and tried to hug her, partly to comfort her and partly because he also needed comforting. She put her arms round him but continued to cry and didn't speak. Her tears rolled down onto his

9

bare arms and legs and he too began to cry. It was then that Elias came into the house. Mama lifted Winstone off her lap and very gently handed him over to the old man. Elias took Winstone back across the yard to his own house, sat down and cuddled him, rocking back and forth in his chair.

'Papa, where is Papa?' Winstone kept asking between tears, but Grandfather said nothing. The sudden death in his sleep of his eldest and the most reliable of his sons, the one whom he had relied upon to manage the land when he became too old to look after it himself, was more than he could bear.

Everywhere was quiet. The quietness seemed to press in on Winstone, almost smother him as if he had been covered with a thick blanket. He buried his head in Elias's chest and sobbed himself to sleep. After a while Martha appeared at the door and woke him with some milk in a cup and a chapati. It was now nearly mid-day. He had been given no breakfast and needed something to eat. Later on, he was taken back to his house where he saw his father lying in bed. For a moment he was full of joy. There was his father after all! He went over to him and shook his arm.

'Papa, Papa,' he said eagerly. 'Wake up, wake up! It's day-time!'

But his father's eyelids remained closed. Gone were those twinkling eyes and the smiling face, and the body never moved. It was as if he didn't know Winstone was there.

A day or two passed and then many people appeared at Elias's house. Winstone recognised his aunts and uncles and his two cousins but there were many he did not know. They all looked solemn and spoke in whispers and they seemed too absorbed in the death of their relative to take much notice of him. He sat listless and forlorn in a corner by himself, mesmerised by the press of people. Then Mama found him and picked him up in her arms. She said nothing. Her face was expressionless, but she hugged him tightly, almost as if she was frightened of losing him. Many people were wailing. The noise of their crying frightened him. Eventually he became so upset he was taken away and cared for by somebody he didn't know. People stayed around for four days. He was so confused he didn't remember much of the funeral. He recalled people sitting around on the ground. Sometimes a person got up and talked to the rest who listened in silence. He remembered people going over to his Papa's body, bending down and touching it one by one. The sight startled him. Although people were touching him Papa still didn't wake up. When everyone present had touched the body, Mama carried Winstone over to do the same, but he screamed and struggled in her arms and held his hands up in the air, crying, "No, no, no", until she knelt down and holding his arm forced him to touch the body. Now he cried inconsolably. He remembered everyone standing round his father's body. All of a sudden, he was frightened. What was going to happen to his beloved father? Then to his horror he saw Papa gently laid in a big hole dug in the ground and covered with earth. It seemed his father had gone forever. Would he never come back? Would he never see those twinkling eyes and that warm smile again? He was sobbing his heart out.

Then his mother said Papa was dead and had gone to live with Jesus, but Winstone didn't understand what that meant. Papa was still here but buried in the ground, so how could he have gone to live with someone else? His crying upset his mother and she too began to weep bitterly. He remembered people starting to sing while some came over to try to comfort her. One of them picked him up and carried him away and, exhausted from grieving, he must have fallen asleep.

CHAPTER TWO

On the last evening of the funeral, when everybody had been fed and all the mourners had returned home, Catherine and John and his daughter Petra came over and sat with Delia to try to work out what the future held for her. Winstone was glad to have Petra's company. She was two years older than him and since there were no other youngsters around, he regarded her like an older sister. They went outside to play hide and seek and for a time it took his mind off missing his father.

Delia was drained. She tried to put on a brave face but every now and again broke into weeping.

'It's been such a shock,' she said. 'It has all happened so quickly. One minute, Jeremiah was here and the next he was gone, and I shall never see him again. We kissed and said our prayers together as we always do before we go to sleep. Everything was so utterly normal. If only I had stayed awake, I might have been able to do something to save his life. If only I could have given him some comfort in his dying moments. If only I could have said goodbye.'

Catherine sat next to her and held her hand. Delia had always been such a happy, smiling person, carefree yet with love for those around her and always ready to comfort others and to lend a helping hand. Now her face, once so radiant, was drawn and grey and her joyfulness snuffed out like a candle. As a nurse, Catherine was familiar with death, but she had not experienced the effect death could have on those left behind. She felt at a loss as to what to say.

'I think I would not have been so shocked if Jeremiah had suffered a slow death,' Delia continued, 'but to wake up in the morning and find him lying dead next to me was – well, it was just incomprehensible. I thought he was fast asleep, and I tried to wake him. I turned to hug him. Then I realised his body was cold and he wasn't breathing. For a long time, I couldn't believe it. I thought I must be hallucinating. I tried shaking him as if he would come alive. Then I sat on the bed stunned. Nothing made sense. How could such a thing happen? It was beyond imagination. Then I went over and called Elias and Martha because I thought I was not in my right mind and I wanted them to say it was all a bad dream. But it wasn't. When they saw Jeremiah they too were stunned. I thought Martha was going to faint. Her face was so white. Then came floods of tears and she kissed his forehead time and time again saying, "My, son, my son, oh my son." Elias said nothing. There was his favourite son, the one he relied upon to maintain and develop the farm, lying there dead. He stood by the body for a long time then went outside. It's unseemly for a man to be seen crying. I think he must have gone away to hide his tears.

And then did you hear those neighbours at the funeral? There was that group of them discussing whether or not Jeremiah had died of AIDS. AIDS! What a disgrace! How could they think such thing of my dear husband?' Delia wiped her eyes. 'I'm sorry I'm crying again,' she said. 'I can't help it.'

Catherine put her arm round her. 'Take no notice of that ill-informed gossip my dear. It's common knowledge that AIDS doesn't kill overnight. It's a long, drawn out illness. I know what bewilderment you must be facing. The abrupt death of a loved one is something we never imagine will happen to us. No, Jeremiah must have died of sudden heart failure. It is a terrible thing to happen. Sadly, it seems it is not uncommon in men of his age and we don't really know why it happens. I know you must be terribly shocked. I feel so sad for you, but it's good you can talk about it and it's not shameful to cry. It's all part of the healing process. I am just so glad we're here to listen to you and comfort you. There may never be anyone as close to you as Jeremiah was, but you can be sure we love you and will do all we can to support you and little Winstone as you face life without our dear brother.'

'Tell me,' asked John, 'what do you think the future now holds for you Delia?'

'That's not the sort of thing you should bother Delia with now,' Catherine said.

'I know,' replied John, 'but neither of us are going to be staying here and we need to know what we can do to help before we leave.'

'I don't know what to think,' said Delia. She paused for a moment and tried to gather her thoughts. 'I can't believe I will ever marry again,' she said. 'I don't think I would find anyone as dear to me as Jeremiah.' She brightened a little. 'I'm just so thankful I've got Winstone. He reminds me so much of his father and I love him so much. I think he's going to be clever. I want him to have the best possible education and have him make his way in the world. That's what Jeremiah would have wanted I feel sure. He would have been so proud of him.'

She sighed, held her head in her hands for a moment and thought about the immediate future. 'I feel I shall have to stand in for Jeremiah. There's no place for slackers in a family of farmers. It's a family effort. Those twins are hopeless, and your father will struggle to run the farm without Jeremiah's help. It's the physical help your father will need in his old age. When Winstone gets a little older he will be able to help out in the school holidays. You know how much he loves the farm. I'm thinking too, that we ought to have our own stall at the market rather than getting others to sell our produce for us. We could make more money that way.'

'That's good thinking,' said John. 'And when I've got some free time, perhaps at the week-ends, I can drive over and help, and if I bring Petra with me she'll be good company for Winstone and give Miriam a bit of a break from looking after both kids and the baby all the time.'

'It's a blessing you have that car,' said Catherine. 'I remember father's face when you first turned up with it. He never imagined a son of his would have his own car! Do you remember how he begged you to give him a ride and then how terrified he was when you went fast enough to overtake a bicycle! And how the neighbours came to view the very first car in the neighbourhood? My goodness, how they admired you, John!'

Delia felt very isolated and alone once Catherine and Petra and her father had departed. At the funeral she had had to concentrate on her role as the widow and somehow, surrounded by so many people, she felt shielded from her own thoughts. John and Catherine had been a great support to her. She needed their company, their understanding and their empathy. She knew there would be no support from the twins and Elias and Martha were themselves too upset to offer any immediate comfort. Now, with everybody gone and

Winstone in bed, her thoughts crowded in on her. She shrank at the realisation of the burdens she faced - responsibility for the old people, responsibility for the farm, caring for a child trying to come to terms with the loss of his beloved father and dealing with her two wayward brothers-in-law. It had been hard enough for Jeremiah to get them to pull their weight on the farm. In a society where women are considered inferior to men, it seemed it would be a hopeless task for her. The prospect of it all was daunting. Jeremiah had been her mainstay ever since she had married him. What had been a happy, carefree life a few days ago had dissolved into chaos, into something she was not the least bit prepared for.

For a few nights Winstone was too upset to sleep alone. Buried under that earth, it dawned on him that he would never see his father again. Something he didn't understand had taken him away forever. Even Mama seemed changed. She was pale and unhappy, and she seemed to need little Winstone as much as he needed her. He spent long hours in her arms. She held him close and talked to him gently, stroked his head to comfort him and sang him songs. Sometimes she cried gently and Winstone would cry with her, their tears mingling in their close embrace. Then the time came when he returned to his own bed. On that first night he had not slept for long before he was awoken by angry sounds from the living room. Wide awake, he was shaking with fear. He recognised the voices of his twin uncles, Matthew and Mark. There was an argument going on, all the while getting louder. Voices rose to a crescendo. Above the brothers' voices he could hear his mother. Her voice was high pitched and horse.

She was screaming at the men in-between sobs saying, "Get out, go, go!"

Never before had Winstone experienced such a commotion in his home. Then there was banging, such hard-menacing blows it seemed. Blow after blow and the men screaming in fury, first in the house, then outside. He heard their footsteps tramping across the yard. The door of the house slammed shut and the key was turned in the lock. His mother was still sobbing. Terrified at what had gone on, Winstone cowed under the bed clothes. Peace had returned to the house except for his mother's crying. Still very frightened, he was desperate for his mother's company. It was dark in his bedroom but he could see a chink of light from the hurricane lamp in the living room. Feverishly he slipped out of bed, his little heart racing, and made for the living room door. His mother sat on the floor, her head in her hands. Lying in front of her was his father's long wooden club which he kept in case of intruders. He had never seen his father use it. In fact, he had never seen it anywhere but where it was kept in a corner of the room.

'Mama! Mama!' shouted Winstone as he rushed towards her. Now he was crying. His mother gathered him up in her arms and together they sat on the floor. They cried together for a long time. His mother kept saying, "My son, oh my son, my son, how I love you," and it seemed as if she was hugging him tighter than she had ever hugged him before.

Winstone must have fallen asleep in his mother's arms for when he awoke, he was in his own bed. The events of the previous evening had tired him out. He had slept longer than usual for the morning was already far advanced and the sun had risen high in the sky.

The room was flooded with light and he could hear the chickens clucking out in the yard. Mama was no longer in bed. She must have got up already to prepare breakfast, yet apart from the chickens he could hear no other sound outside. There was no clatter of pots and pans and the swish of water as Mama washed them out, which she did every morning before bringing him his drink of milk. Something was not quite right. He got down out of bed and went into the living room. There was no sign of Mama there. Then he went out across the grass to the kitchen, his feet cold and wet from dew not yet burnt off by the sun. But there was no fire lit in the hearth to heat water and the pots and pans were left unwashed where they had been the previous day. For a moment Winstone stood dazed by the stillness around him. Where could Mama have gone? He could never remember a time when she had not helped him out of bed and given him a warm drink of milk to start the day. With his father gone he needed her more than ever.

Suddenly he was overcome with fear. Had that same thing that had taken his father away taken his mother as well? In panic he started to shout "Mama! Mama!" He ran back to the house, tears streaming down his face shouting for his Mama as he searched in every corner, but she was nowhere to be seen. Apart from his crying, the house was silent and deserted. Then thoroughly distressed he ran as fast as his legs would take him to Grandfather's house still crying out for his mother. Elias met him in the doorway. He looked surprised. He swept him up in his arms and asked him what the matter was, but by that time Winstone was too overcome with sobbing to utter a word. Martha heard the commotion. She had just finished washing clothes and came hurriedly from the bushes where she had laid them out to dry. Try as they might, they couldn't calm the little boy. His sobbing was so intense his whole body was shaking. He was red in the face and he was coughing and choking in an attempt to catch his breath.

Still crying, they carried him back to his home and called for his mother, but there was no reply. The grandparents looked puzzled. They would not usually enter their son's house without first being invited in.

Martha was hesitant. 'I don't really like to, but I think I ought to go in. What do you say Elias?'

'I don't know what else you can do.'

Martha cautiously went inside. Elias followed her and stood by the door, holding Winstone in his arms. Like many rural African homes, it was built of mud-brick walls with a corrugated-iron roof and was sparsely furnished with just a table and chairs, a cupboard and chests of drawers, a couple of beds, a writing desk, a calendar on the wall advertising a haulage firm, the *litungu*, shutters on unglazed windows, no curtains, and a hurricane lamp to provide light when darkness came. Had an intruder come during the night there would have been signs of a disturbance but everything seemed to be in order, except for the club lying on the floor and that her daughter-in-law was no longer there.

'I can't think why that club is lying on the floor when it's usually kept in the corner of the room,' commented Martha. 'That's not usual.' She moved into the other rooms. 'A few of Delia's belongings seem to be missing,' she called to Elias. 'I wonder why that is?'

'It's a mystery,' said Elias when his wife joined him back at the door. 'I'm bothered the club is not in its usual place. She can't have been attacked, can she?' The grandparents looked grave. It was not like Winstone's mother to go out into the fields and leave Winstone alone in the house. Martha took Winstone in her arms and went back to her home while Elias picked up the stave he always carried with him and went to search the farm and the land around.

It was late morning when he returned. Elias had found no trace of his daughter-in-law. The twins had been out in the fields early but they said they had not seen Delia and neither had any of the neighbours. Elias did however notice that Mark walked with a limp.

'Hurt your leg, have you?' asked Elias.

'Oh, it was nothing much,' replied Mark. 'I tripped and fell. Must have twisted it somehow.'

It was obvious Delia was nowhere around. In the close-knit community in which they lived she would have been seen by someone if she had left the farm, and if she had left the farm the only other place she would be likely to have gone, would be the market. That would perhaps explain why some of her belongings were no longer in the house. Yet it was unlikely she would have gone without taking Winstone with her, or more likely, leaving him with his grandparents, because the market was twenty minutes' walk away. It was already early afternoon and the market stalls would begin to pack up, and if she had gone to the market on her own, she should be on her way back by now. Nevertheless, Elias felt the situation was serious enough to get out his bike and cycle into town in search of her. He might meet her on the way. On the other hand, she might have had an accident or be detained somewhere. The market attracted customers from a wide area around. An unaccompanied woman in a crowd of strangers, was always vulnerable.

It was almost dark by the time Elias returned. He was weary and dispirited. His search had been in vain. Many people in Cheptais knew Delia. They knew her for her good looks and her cheery smile, but none had seen her at the market or around the shops. Elias mentioned the club he had found on the floor, but the police knew of no incident that might have involved Delia. No young woman had reported being attacked, nor being in an accident nor registered sick in the health centre that day.

Winstone was fed in his grandparent's house. He had cried for his mother most of the day and however much she tried, Martha had been unable to comfort him. The club on the floor bothered Elias and Martha. By bedtime Winstone had calmed down and ceased crying. They asked him very gently whether he remembered anything happening in the house.

'My uncles came,' he said.

'When did they come?' asked Martha.

'I don't know. I was asleep.'

'But if you were asleep how did you know they came?' asked Elias.

'I was in bed. I woke up. There was banging and... and shouting and... and Mama was crying.'

'And did you go to sleep again?' asked Elias.

'No. I was so frightened; I ran to Mama.'

'And were your uncles still there?' asked Martha.

'No. I heard them go.'

That evening the grandparents sat with heavy hearts.

'Those boys,' said Elias, 'they should never have burst in on Delia like that when she is alone with no man to protect her. They know such behaviour is unacceptable in our society. What, you think they attacked her? Is that why she was crying? Is that what the noise was about? Is that what woke Winstone?'

Martha rocked to-and-fro in her chair. 'It's hurtful to say it of my sons,' she said, 'but I'm really afraid of those boys, you know. Left on their own, there's no limit to the mischief they might get up to. Jeremiah had a way of keeping them in order. That's something Delia would never be able to do. They take precious little notice of you Elias and they certainly wouldn't of a woman. You must confront them in the morning and find out what they were up to.'

Elias did not look forward to challenging the twins. He was an elderly man - a *mzee* - and a *mzee* should receive respect, the more so since he was their father. Yet he knew they had little respect for him, and he also knew they would take offence if he questioned them. However, this was a serious matter and, as their father and head of the family, it was his responsibility to find out what had taken place.

When he found them, they were eating breakfast in Matthew's house. He stood in the doorway. They invited him in, but Elias stayed where he was. This was not a social occasion. He had come to reprimand them, and it was better done from a distance. Elias came straight to the point.

'I have come to ask you what happened in the evening before Delia disappeared,' he said in his sternest voice.

'Nothing much happened that evening,' Matthew answered. 'We didn't know she had disappeared until next morning, did we?'

'Yet you saw her that evening,' Elias persisted.

'Well, we saw her around in the afternoon, didn't we?' Mark said, looking at Matthew.

'Yes,' said Matthew. 'She was weeding between the cabbages and she had Winstone helping her.'

'Yes,' said Elias, 'but you went around to her house in the evening.'

'No, we never!' Mark said firmly. 'Did we Matthew?'

'No, we sat at your place Mark, playing cards.'

'That's not true,' said Elias. 'I have evidence you were there and causing a disturbance and you know very well it's taboo to enter a woman's house when she is alone in the evening even if she was to invite you in.'

The twins laughed. 'Come on Dad, what evidence have you got?'

'According to Winstone there was a great row going on and he heard your voices,' said Elias.

'According to Winstone, ay? Heard our voices?' chided Mark. 'Come off it. That kid must've been dreaming. He's probably having nightmares now his father's gone. Poor kid, it must've been an awful shock for him. No wonder he's disturbed. You'll be telling us in a moment he saw us.'

'No, he didn't see you,' said Elias. 'He said he was too scared by the rumpus to come out of his bedroom.'

'There you are,' Matthew said scornfully. 'What did I tell you, it was all a bad dream. He just imagined it. After all, he's only a kid. He could imagine all sorts of things if his mind was disturbed.'

'So why did he find his mother crying when he got out of bed? What could have upset her if it hadn't been for you two? And why was Jeremiah's club laying on the floor?'

'We don't know,' retorted Mark. 'That's her business. Nothing to do with us.'

'I don't know why you are accusing us,' Matthew said. 'Why would we want to mess with her? We're not womanisers. You know damn well no woman has ever taken any interest in us. As I said, we were at Mark's place playing cards and having a drink or two. You don't believe us, do you? But if you had come around for yourself you could have joined us.'

Matthew's voice was mocking. Elias was nettled. His sons knew he didn't drink alcohol and they knew he didn't approve of their drinking or playing cards.

'No, you're right,' said Elias, 'I don't believe you for one moment. You two can never be relied upon to tell the truth. But sooner or later the truth will out and then we will know who's right!'

It was devastating losing the eldest son at such a young age but the disappearance of his wife so soon after and leaving the little boy all alone to fend for himself, was more than Elias and Martha could bear. The only course of action left to them was to try to contact Delia's parents. As is usually the case in Africa, when a girl marries, she becomes absorbed into the husband's family and ties with the in-laws become distant, and in this society in particular there was often animosity between the two families.

Elias had never had much to do with Delia's family after his son married. There had been some dissent over the terms of the dowry paid to Delia's parents and so each family had kept themselves very much to themselves. Delia's family lived some distance away, further than Elias could cycle, so the following day he sent a messenger to inform them that their daughter had left her home shortly after her husband's death, and to find out whether they knew of her whereabouts. The messenger returned saying her parents were extremely upset that Delia had disappeared but had no news of her. Winstone's grandparents were unconvinced by the reply. It seemed to them that she might have returned to her home after all. Tribal laws decree that children belong to the father's family whatever the circumstances and she would have had no option but to leave Winstone with his grandparents rather than take him with her wherever she may have gone.

Then a day or two later two of Delia's brothers turned up at the farm. They demanded to know what had happened to Delia. They were suspicious. If Delia had fled after her husband's death she would almost certainly have returned to her old home. They accused Elias of driving her out of the farm. They even suggested he might have poisoned her and hidden her body.

Elias was furious. 'How dare you accuse me of such evil things,' he shouted. 'I am a simple God-fearing man. Don't you believe I am as upset as you are that my daughter-in-law has vanished? I loved that girl as if she was my own daughter. Don't you think the boy is heart-broken having lost both his father and his mother? What right do you have to come here onto my land and say such a thing? Delia was married into our family, not yours!'

'And married into poverty instead of going to university and getting a decent job,' shouted the eldest one.

'She married out of love not money,' retorted Elias.

'She was too good to be married to a farmer,' said the younger brother. 'She had no future here as a farmer's wife rearing chickens, toiling in the fields and milking cows when she could have had a career in an office wearing decent clothes and married to someone who had a good position in life and not a farmer's son. That's what she was cut out for.'

'You never came near her after she married,' said the old man. 'You ignored her. None of you came to see the child after he was born and no one came to her husband's funeral. How do you think she felt about that? Yet she was the sweetest, kindest person you could imagine and what's more she was a happy individual, not grasping and belligerent like you!'

'Well,' countered the older of the two, making towards Jeremiah's house, 'if nothing else, we have come to collect our sister's belongings.'

'You will do no such thing!' said Elias sharply. 'The boy is in there and he is not to be disturbed and neither do you have any authority to take away things that belong to our family! In any case you have no right to be on my land uninvited.'

Elias was a small man and although elderly he was still strong. Next moment the two brothers felt the full strength of Elias's stave across their backs and then across the back of their legs. Unarmed and reeling from pain they turned and ran off. That was the last the old man saw of them.

CHAPTER THREE

Caring for Winstone became a burden for his grandparents and one they had not wished to take on. Having reared six children of their own, they had looked forward to their more mature years being free from childcare. Miriam, John's pregnant wife, could hardly be expected to look after another child and in any case, Winstone was so attached to the farm and his home, he would not have settled to an urban life. Then again neither Crispin with his kind of job nor Catherine as a student, were in a position to look after him.

After the passing of his eldest son and the disappearance of his daughter-in-law, it was Elias who once again in his advancing years had to turn to and manage the land since the twins were incapable of looking after it themselves. This meant Martha was left largely on her own to care for the troubled youngster, still grieving the loss of his parents. Whereas Jeremiah's phlegmatic nature restrained him from berating Matthew and Mark when they did not pull their weight, Elias was not so tolerant. When a son has been circumcised and builds and lives in his own house, the parents do not have the right to enter it unless invited, yet there were many occasions when Elias took his stave and beat the twins out of bed and drove them out to the fields. It led to resentment and abuse by the boys, not only oral abuse but on occasions physical abuse as well and at times Elias had to defend himself with the stave he carried.

'If only those boys were married like other young men of their age,' Elias used to say to his wife. 'Wives might have made them more responsible and more congenial to others, perhaps even made them less selfish. It might also have given them a degree of motivation when it comes to working on the farm and perhaps even made them more respectful.'

And Martha would reply in despair, 'Yes, I know, but it's because of their reputation in the community. They've never found girls who would marry them and while they remain as they are, they never will. Unless they change their ways, they'll be a burden to us for the rest of our lives.'

Indeed, their notoriety was such that they had few friends and those they had were drinking partners who congregated in an old tobacco drying house at the far end of the village where home-made liquor flowed liberally, with the result they were often too drunk to walk home and had to sleep the night there.

When his father had been alive, the twins had been of little trouble to Winstone but once his mother had gone, they began to tease him viciously. It was as if they were taking revenge for her disappearance. It was cruel the way they treated Winstone. They would offer him something nice to eat and then snap it away before he could take it. Or they would hide behind a tree and then frighten him by jumping out and shouting as he passed. Sometimes they would purposely knock into him so that he fell on the ground and then they would walk off laughing. More frightening was when they twisted his arm behind his back or put their hands round his neck feigning to strangle him.

For Winstone, what had once been an idyllic childhood, now became a nightmare. He lacked love and he lacked security. Because of the twin's behaviour he was scared to go out into the fields, and when he did so he stayed close to Elias for protection. The old man was not particularly pleased to have Winstone following him around all the time and although he still did some weeding, his grandfather never praised his efforts.

When his father was alive Winstone roamed freely around the farm. Now he felt constrained. He kept a wary eye on the twins and stayed out of sight as much as he could, fearing they would come and tease him. When Grandfather was out on his bike, he sought the company of his grandmother for safety or stayed close to his old home, either playing with the chickens or going and opening his mother's desk to look at her drawings. There were many drawings and almost all were of things around the farm: the chickens, the interior of the kitchen with its pots and pans and smoke curling up from the fire, or the grain stores, big round wicker woven containers on four little legs and topped with a thatched "coolie hat". Then there were drawings from the fields. Not all the drawings were in pencil. Some were coloured in crayon or water colours. The one he liked best was of a field of sun flowers, brilliant yellow with green stems and leaves. In another she had used delicate shades to paint a butterfly. Another painting depicted the foothills of Mount Elgon with clumps of trees, little meadows and the cultivated fields in-between.

Winstone sought solace in these works of art. He was safe in the house during the daytime and slept with his grandparents at night until he was deemed to be old enough to look after himself. The pictures helped him remember the happy times, singing by the light of the hurricane lamp, sitting in the kitchen while food was being cooked or helping to feed the hens. They kept the memory of his mother fresh in his mind. At other times he went to the wardrobe where some of his mother's clothes, and the yellow scarf she always wore when she was working round the house, were hanging. The scent she wore still lingered in them and it reminded him of all those times she had tucked him up in bed and kissed him good night, leaving that faint aroma on his cheek. Those were the happy days. Often, he stood there alone, sobbing for want of his mother and father. Here he could weep in private for his grandparents got annoyed if he wept in their house and told him to grow up and be a brave boy. At other times he went and stood by his father's grave and talked to him hoping that by some miracle he would reply. The memory of his father was so fresh in his mind he still believed one day he would return to live with him.

Then one night, Jeremiah did come to him. It was in a dream. Winstone was in the yard feeding the chickens and suddenly his father was there standing beside him. 'Papa!' Winstone exclaimed.

His father smiled at him, a twinkle still in his eyes.

'One day my son', he said, 'you will be famous'.

And then he was gone and Winstone woke up. Brief though it was, Winstone from that time on knew his father had not deserted him. It warmed his heart. It was his secret. It was a dream he would keep to himself and it was a dream he would never forget. As time went by Winstone tried to copy some of his mother's drawings. He didn't have the courage to use crayons or to take up a paint brush, so he kept to pencils and there were many of them in the drawer. At first his efforts yielded little, but he copied the same drawing time and time again until, at last, he produced something akin to the original. His grandparents never bothered about the time he spent away from them. They knew he was somewhere safe and were relieved he kept himself occupied.

It was unusual for a child to be on its own within a family setting. Most families had four or five children or more, and many had cousins nearby. They all played together in a large group. No child was ever alone; Winstone's situation was exceptional.

Elias was aware of Winstone's loneliness and one Sunday when he was a little older, he said, 'I thought you might like to go to church with me this morning. You will meet a lot of people there and maybe some children as well.'

Being confined to the farm for most of the time, Winstone was glad to go for walks and explore new places. Elias abandoned his workday clothes and wore his best jacket and trousers when he went to church with a brown trilby hat adorned with a grey silk band. Winstone thought his grandfather looked very smart.

The church Elias attended was in the next community. It was a long walk between fields of maize and sunflowers so high Winstone couldn't see over them. Now and again, they disturbed birds hidden among the stems. They flew up in fright, startling Winstone. There were a couple of streams to be crossed, each with a plank so that you could walk over them dry shod. The fields of maize and sunflowers gave way to meadows where low, moisture-loving plants grew in abundance, speckling the grass with a cloth of white and yellow flowers. The air was fresh and warm. Winstone was invigorated by the smell of rich damp earth mingled with the fragrance of flowers which rose up from the meadows and he breathed in deeply as he strode to keep up with his grandfather. It was good to be in the countryside. He loved the clumps of tall grasses dancing in the breeze, the call of birds and the occasional lowing of cattle. To him it was music to the ears and calming to the senses.

'Why do we go to church, Grandfather?'

'So that we can praise God and pray to Jesus,' came the reply.

Winstone was elated. Mama had said Papa had gone to live with Jesus and if Jesus came to church, he would surely bring Papa with him. The church was a long, low building with brick walls and a tiled roof. He had not seen a building quite like that before. It was set in a broad expanse of grass surrounded by trees.

'Do you see that tree standing over there?' Grandfather was pointing to a tree standing in isolation in the middle of the grass. Winstone followed his gaze. 'You were christened under that tree when you were born.'

Grandfather knew most of the congregation and on arrival there was a great deal of hand shaking. People shook hands whenever they met and again when they said goodbye. Most of them bent down and shook hands with Winstone as well and that made him feel very grown up. He enjoyed the singing. He loved it when the congregation swayed and sang lustily to the accompaniment of a drum, but since the service was in Swahili and not his own language, he could understand very little. Elias had only just started to teach him a few words of the language most people spoke to overcome the problem of the several tribal tongues commonly in use in the area where they lived. However, the name of Jesus was mentioned by the pastor many times and he even mentioned Papa. It sent a thrill through Winstone.

Jesus must surely be somewhere amongst all the people attending the service. He kept looking around for Jesus and Papa, but he couldn't see them anywhere.

When prayers were said Winstone went into his own little world and prayed fervently over and over again saying, "Please God, send my Mama back to me," until he was shaking with emotion. He pleaded with God that she was not dead whatever his grandmother said.

He did not like it when the service finished. Then the congregation stood in groups chatting. They took pity on the poor little orphan, patting him on the head and giving him nice things to eat to compensate for his loss. He didn't need to be patronised and he certainly didn't need to be pitied. What he needed more than anything else was to be loved. Neither his grandparents nor the churchgoers put their arms round him or gave him a kiss and he dare not ask them to love him because he knew instinctively, to be meaningful, love had to be given freely, unconditionally and spontaneously.

Before they left for home the pastor came up and shook hands with Elias and Winstone. The pastor was a tall elderly man with a head of almost white hair, bushy white eyebrows, a kindly face and graceful demeanour, remarkably like one of the ancients, lacking only a long white beard. Winstone stood between them clearly dejected. Bending down to him, Grandfather enquired whether something was the matter.

'Where is my Papa?' he asked.

Elias and the pastor were perplexed by his question.

Grandfather frowned. 'But Winstone, you know that your father has died.'

'I know, but Mama said Papa has gone to live with Jesus and the man kept talking about Jesus and I couldn't see Jesus or Papa anywhere.'

The pastor shook his head.

'The poor child,' he said to Elias. 'He must be missing his father terribly and church has only caused confusion. Let me see if I can explain to him.' He took Winstone over to a bench and sat down with him. Very gently he explained, 'You see, Winstone, your father is living with Jesus, but he is living with Jesus in heaven. Heaven is not here where we are, but we can speak to Jesus when we pray to him because he can hear our prayers. God is also in heaven and he can hear our prayers as well. God is like a father to all of us. So sometimes we call him 'Papa' instead of calling him God.'

Winstone thought the pastor was a kind man but he hadn't given him a hug and he hadn't brought his father back to him. When they arrived home, he said to his grandfather that he didn't want to go to church again if his father wasn't there.

Because his grandparents were elderly and beyond childbearing, it was understandable that their friends were also elderly, with grown-up children, and so Winstone had no youngsters to play with. It was only when his cousins arrived from Eldoret that he lost his sense of isolation. Winstone was reserved but Petra and Michael were boisterous, out-going individuals, bursting into his surroundings with unrestrained energy. Winstone's demeanour changed instantly as he was swept up in their feverish activities. He loved their company, their joyfulness and their sense of fun. The old metal wheelbarrow was one of their favourite toys.

'I'm in charge,' Petra would say. She was bossy, inventive and at times impatient. 'Sit in the wheelbarrow one behind the other,' she would command the boys. 'I'm going to take you for a ride.' Then taking the handles she would tear round the trees and bushes turning sharp corners as if she was a racing car driver. Sometimes she turned a corner too fast, tipping the boys on the ground where they fell laughing in a mangled heap. At other times Petra sat in the barrow herself while the boys each took a handle. They never got far however because of their lack of co-ordination which caused the wheelbarrow to crash into trees or overturn.

Another favourite game was for Petra to persuade her father to lay a blindfold trail. They had to hide out of sight while he took a ball of string, tied one end to a tree trunk then wound the string round other trees and bushes, under low branches and through undergrowth. Petra was always the first to be blindfolded and guided by her father to the string at the first tree. Then, with one hand free to feel her way forward and the other holding the string she navigated her way to the end of the trail. Then it was Winstone's turn. Petra laughed when he couldn't get past an obstacle or tripped and lost his balance. Finally, it was Michael's turn but since he was the youngest both Petra and Winstone helped him through the course. Winstone felt a great sense of freedom on these occasions. His twin uncles never dared to intervene when they were playing together, for they knew their older brother would come after them.

Elias and Martha were also more relaxed when John was back at home. Mealtimes were joyous occasions when they all sat round the table together, the three children, John and his parents and later on Miriam and the baby. John always brought with him food from town. It was the kind of groceries which were not available in the countryside. Martha enjoyed preparing meals with new and exciting ingredients she had not used before and Winstone looked forward to exploring new tastes and flavours.At other times Catherine came to stay, usually at a weekend when she had time off from her training. Her presence made Winstone particularly happy. She was the one member of the family who understood the intensity of loss experienced by Winstone now that he was an orphan. When she was with him, she tried to take the place of his mother. He loved the hugs she gave him. It made him feel he was really wanted by someone and he loved it when she sang to him as he was tucked up in bed, just as his mother used to do. They went for walks together. As much as he loved the farm, he enjoyed a walk out in the countryside, walking along footpaths and over streams to explore places he had never seen before. In particular, he was glad of the freedom of being away from the twins. Sometimes they walked down to the river to see boys swimming and splashing about in the water. At other times they walked along the murram road towards the school Winstone would attend when he was older, or down to where the springs were where children gathered to collect drinking water and then carried it home to their families in buckets carefully perched on their heads.

Sometimes in the rainy season when they couldn't walk outside, Catherine came over to Winstone's house and read stories to him, or else they looked through some of his mother's paintings and drawings. Catherine was surprised at his drawing ability. He was now approaching five, yet his proficiency was more like that of a nine-year- old.

'Why do you always draw with a pencil?' she asked. 'Why don't you sometimes use crayons or paints?'

'That's because the crayons have got worn down now and I can't use them anymore. I can't sharpen them because Grandfather won't let me use a knife. He said it's too dangerous, and I am afraid to use paint in case I spill the water and spoil what I'm doing.'

'What you need,' Catherine observed, 'is a pencil sharpener. Have you never seen one? They're very small. They have a blade, but you can't cut yourself. You just turn it on the end of the crayon, and it cuts a new point beautifully. I'll bring you one when I next come to visit, and I'll also bring a special container that you can put water in without it spilling.'

Winstone smiled delightedly. How kind my aunt is he thought to himself.

'I wish you always lived here,' he said.

'Well, that's not possible,' said Catherine, 'but I'll come as often as I can, and one day when you're a little older and I've finished my training we'll go on trips together. Maybe we can go to see the elephants and lions and rhinoceros on the plains and other animals which you never see here, and perhaps I'll take you to see a big city, or even to the ocean.'

Winstone thought those were wonderful ideas and wished he could grow up quickly.

'I would really like to draw a big, big rhinoceros,' he said.

'What do you want to do when you grow up?' Catherine asked.

'I want to be an artist like my mother or maybe a long-distance lorry driver like Uncle Crispin.'

They laughed at the thought: two entirely different lifestyles.

'Well, I like it when Uncle John takes me in his car, and I think it must be so much fun to drive a really big lorry.'

'But roads in the countryside aren't built for big lorries so how can you know what they're like?'

'Oh, I know what they're like,' Winstone said with conviction. 'There's one on that calendar on the wall. Look, it's a really big one with eight wheels and Uncle John has only four on his car and the driver sits much higher than my uncle so he can see right over everybody.'

Catherine's next visit to her parents coincided with Winstone's fifth birthday. Birthdays were not usually celebrated in the family. In some communities where people had still not learnt to read or write, no records were kept of birthdays and often children did not know how old they were. But this family knew when Winstone was born since it was the day of his parents wedding anniversary. Winstone had forgotten Catherine's promise so when she laid a beautifully wrapped parcel in front of him, he was surprised. He was tempted to rip open the paper, but Martha stopped him, saying that such beautiful paper was rare in these parts and ought to be preserved. Instead, she gave Winstone scissors, so he could carefully cut the ribbon and take off the wrapping paper without tearing it. Then to his surprise and joy out fell a pencil sharpener and not only a pencil sharpener but also a small inkwell with a heavy base to hold water. There was also a pad of artist's paper. Winstone threw his arms around Catherine and hugged her.

'You spoil that boy,' said Martha scornfully. 'Those things must have cost a fortune.'

'No, Mother,' corrected Catherine. 'They're not all that expensive. Besides this boy has got real talent. He needs to be encouraged. He has the makings of an artist.'

'There's not much money in being an artist,' observed Elias dryly. 'He needs to get a good office job when he's older, not fiddle about with paints.'

'That's not true,' Catherine corrected. 'There's a world-wide demand for top paintings of Kenya's animals. The best artists make a small fortune out of their paintings these days.'

Winstone disappeared. He made straight for the desk in his house. There he laid out crayons, paints and the pad and filled the inkwell with water. He picked up the pencil sharpener and turned it in the end of one of the crayons. To his amazement thin shavings of wood curled out of the sharpener and fell to the desk-top and when he pulled it out, the crayon had a perfect point to it. What was more, there was a lovely fresh smell of shaven wood. He put the crayon to his nose and breathed in deeply. Filled with enthusiasm he did not stop until all the crayons had been sharpened. He removed a sheet of paper from the pad and laid it carefully on the desk. Then he took the calendar down from the wall, laid it on the desk in front of him and began to draw the outlines of the vehicle. When he had finished, he took up the newly sharpened crayons and began to colour in the drawing exactly as it was in the picture. It took him most of the morning. He was just copying a single sunflower from his mother's painting when he was called across for a meal but when he finished eating, he returned to the picture. This time he used water colours and with tongue hanging out of his mouth in concentration he painted in the colours. It didn't come out quite as expected. He had too much water on his brush to start with and the painting was rather smudged. When he had finished, he put it out to dry and began to draw from memory the parcel as it was when he first received it, using crayons again which he could handle better than paint. The finished picture was not quite as the parcel had been, but it was good enough. With an air of satisfaction he went to join the family and proudly presented his grandparents with the flower painting and Catherine with the parcel drawing.

'Sorry about the smudge,' he said. 'I made a mistake using too much water.'

Martha looked at the painting for a moment then said, 'It's a very good picture for one of your age.'

When Catherine was given her picture, she was surprised how much detail Winstone had remembered even if the parcel wasn't quite its original shape.

'And this picture is for Uncle Crispin when we next see him,' Winstone announced with a flourish.

Grandfather contemplated the picture for a moment. 'You copied this one off the calendar, didn't you?' he said. 'Your uncle sent us these calendars you know, because this is his lorry, the one he drives. He'll be very pleased to have this picture drawn by his five-year-old nephew.'

When Winstone had gone to bed that evening and Catherine and her parents were sitting alone Elias commented, 'I could never draw like that. I can't put down on paper what I see with my eyes. I am perplexed that this five-year-old can do something that at my age I am still unable to do. I find it remarkable. It seems he must have inherited his ability from his mother, certainly not from us nor his father.'

CHAPTER FOUR

Life changed completely for Winstone when he started school. Having had virtually no contact with children of his own age apart from his cousins, he was now surrounded by new friends. He still needed love but the grieving and isolation he felt after the death of his parents receded for a time. Instead, his mind was occupied with the excitement of the new environment he was entering. He was on a par with everyone in his class since they were all new to school and that developed his self-confidence. Being away from the tyranny of his twin uncles renewed his sense of freedom and walking to school without being accompanied by adults enhanced his self-esteem.

Meeting children from poorer backgrounds made him realise that his family was relatively well off. Unlike some children attending school, Winstone was not short of food. Furthermore, Elias's modest income from the land enabled Martha to purchase a new school uniform for him and even a pair of underpants, whereas some families struggled to acquire the obligatory blue shirt and shorts, whether new or second hand. Winstone was proud of his uniform and thought he looked very smart wearing it. Until then all his garments had been ill fitting, badly worn and much mended hand-me-downs from his father and his uncles when they were young. Now he was wearing crisp new clothes which fitted perfectly.

He knew the way to school since he had walked it many times with Catherine. He was fortunate that school was only a quarter of an hour from his home. Some children lived so far away they had to walk for nearly an hour to get there. Carrying a pencil, a pen and a notebook, he walked barefoot because his grandparents could not afford to buy him shoes. Since he had always walked barefoot this was no hardship. Many other pupils also lacked shoes. Children who did have shoes were instructed to take them off in school so that those without footwear did not feel embarrassed.

When everybody had arrived, the children were told to parade in neat rows by the flagpole while the national anthem was sung and the flag was raised. On this first morning the newcomers stood silent leaving the other children to sing because the words were in Swahili which they had still to learn. However, since the ceremony was repeated every day, it was not long before they all joined in the singing. Once the parade was over those attending school for the first time were shown their classroom. There were no desks in Standard One class; the children sat on the floor. Winstone was horrified. The floor was just dried earth easily turning to dust when the children walked on it. He didn't want his new trousers to get dirty.

The teacher came in.

'What's your name?' he said, pointing at Winstone. He had a big stick and a hard smile.

'Winstone, sir.'

'Why are you standing?'

'I don't want to get my shorts dirty.'

All the other children laughed. Winstone felt embarrassed.

'So, you're too proud to sit, are you? Well, you'll sit Winstone like all the rest of the children and be thankful you've got new shorts and not old ones like some of your classmates. Now let me remind all of you,' he said, addressing the class, 'that when the teacher comes in, you all stand as a sign of respect and you don't sit until I tell you. When I say "Good morning children. How are you?" you reply "Good morning teacher. We're fine thank-you".'

He walked out and came in again. Everybody obediently stood up.

'Good morning children. How are you?'

'Good morning teacher. We are fine thank-you,' everybody replied.

'Welcome to school and your first day of learning'. He then began the lesson,

pointing to the letter "A" on the blackboard. 'Open your notebooks, get out your pencils and write down this letter.'

Not everybody had a notebook. One small boy had neither a pencil nor a notebook. Winstone noticed that those who had no means of writing down the letter looked confused and uncomfortable but instead of chastising them the teacher ignored them.

'This letter is called "A", he said. 'Now say "A" after me.'

Everybody said "A".

'And the letter "A" sounds like this: "aah." 'Now say' "aah".

Everybody said "aah".

'Grandfather,' Winstone asked when he got home, 'why didn't everybody come to school with a pencil and a notebook?'

'I expect because their parents hadn't the money to buy them. When I was at school no-one could afford pencils or paper. We had to write with our fingers on the bare earth we were sitting on.'

'But how will they learn without pencils and paper?' Winstone asked.

'They won't,' Grandfather replied. 'If someone doesn't give them those things they'll probably drop out of school.'

Winstone had enjoyed his first day in Standard One and he couldn't bear the thought that others might not attend classes through lack of basic materials. He realised how lucky he was to have all his mother's pencils, crayons and paints. The next day he put three pencils in his shirt pocket and tore several sheets off his artist's pad, folded them in half, took them to school, gave the paper and a pencil to the boy who had neither and the remaining pencils to two of the girls.

Winstone soon gathered friends around him. He was not shy of going up to people and asking their names. There was a small group of about six boys who all stuck together: Absalom, the boy he gave the paper and pencil to, Andrew, Seth, Kelvin, Hillary and of course Winstone. They all lived near each other so most days they walked to school together. In the morning they walked briskly so as not to be late for parade but on the way home they dawdled. Several girls in the class lived in the same area and often walked home with the boys who amused themselves making faces at them. The girls giggled and whispered to each other about the boys.

A stream had to be crossed. There were stepping-stones in the water but when there had been heavy rain and the water was high, they had to wade across. With the water in full flood, they enjoyed picking up sticks and racing them down-stream. There was a starting point and a finishing point which they marked with large stones on the bank and if the water was flowing fast, they raced along the bank to see who's stick finished first. If they couldn't tell the sticks apart there would be an argument as to who's stick had won.

To impress the girls there was a competition amongst the boys to see who could jump the furthest across the stream where it broadened out. Winstone was not as athletic as the other boys and at his first attempt he fell in. The girls laughed at him. It made him feel ashamed and embarrassed. He went home with a wet uniform and felt the bite of Elias's cane.

During his first few years in school Winstone was not always the best behaved. He had a habit of talking in class when he should have been listening to the teacher or working in silence on an assignment. There were times when he was dragged to the front of the class by the teacher and caned. The headmaster had another form of punishment. He made children who misbehaved kneel in a pose with one arm upright and the other held horizontally for half an hour without moving. As he progressed through the classes Winstone's addiction to talking out of turn led to further punishment. When his class had learnt Swahili, they were no longer allowed to use their native language in school and by Standard Four when English had been learnt there were days when they were not allowed to revert to Swahili. Winstone was careless of these rules and when prefects caught him speaking in the wrong language, he was required to clean out the long-drop toilets or run around the playground as punishment. Nevertheless, there was one punishment Winstone invariably avoided. He was clever, as his mother had predicted. His results were always some of the best in class and he never suffered the indignity of being punished for failing his exams. He was proud of his achievement but was not without feeling for those who failed.

On designated days Winstone's class was required to bring water to school for washing themselves and for cleaning the school since there was no water where the school was built. Neither was there glass in the windows. On dry, windy days dust quickly accumulated inside the building. On wet days bare feet brought in dirt and grit from the footpaths. The school pupils were responsible for keeping the school clean themselves. They had to pick up litter, sweep the floors and wash the furniture, desks and benches on a regular basis under the supervision of the teachers. Bringing water to school was an easy task for Winstone since he merely drew it up from the farm well but for others it meant walking to the nearest spring and filling containers from what was usually no more than a trickle of water. On Fridays, cow dung was brought to school in banana leaves scooped up by pupils from either their own home or from that of a neighbour. At the end of the day water, sand and cow dung were mixed together, smeared over the floor and left to dry to stabilise the earth for the following week's tramping feet. Winstone quite enjoyed this job. To him the mixture had a clean, sweet smell and as he spread it over the earth, he imagined he was preparing the background of a huge picture he would paint over the whole area.

Being at school helped to keep Winstone out of the way of his twin uncles. Yet there were times when they seemed jealous of his academic ability. When Martha and Elias praised him for being clever in the hearing of the twins, they responded by making trouble for their nephew. Textbooks had to be shared between pupils because there were not enough to go around. Yet when it was Winstone's turn to have the books, they disappeared if he left them about. The twins would pick them up and take them home to intimidate Winstone and he would have to beg for their return. Another time at a weekend, they took his school shirt off the bushes after it had been washed and while it was drying, hid it until the Monday morning. There came a time when Winstone couldn't take any more intimidation from these two grown men. Being constantly on the lookout for trouble wearied him. Yet he dare not raise these irritations with his grandparents for fear the twins would cause even more trouble if he complained of their behaviour. He felt defenceless. What could a small boy possibly do in retribution? He began to think of ways he could reap revenge on them. It had to be something that didn't involve force because he was no match for their strength. If he took away their washing while it was drying, it would be obvious he had done it. If he took things from one or other of their houses and hid them, suspicion would immediately fall on him since his grandparents would never enter either house while the twins were elsewhere. It had to be something not directly connected with them, but for which they would get the blame; something carried out discretely.

How he wished his parents were there to protect him. If they were, he would have been spared from his uncles and the need to seek revenge from their torment would not have arisen. He missed his parents more than ever. He hadn't imagined as a small child that when he got older, he would be sitting in the house without them. He would often go to the wardrobe where his mother's dresses and her yellow headscarf still hung. The scent which clung to them still spoke of her presence as did her other belongings such as her drawings and pencils and paints, and they reminded him of happier days.

He could remember clearly his father's face, the bushy eyebrows, those twinkling eyes and his wide smile. But what worried him most was that the recollection of his mother with her softer features had begun to fade as had her mannerisms, the way she walked, her voice and her smile, but the beautiful face, the feature he treasured most, had already slipped from memory. Time was like a thief. Its passage stole away the remembrance of things past, faded memories as colours fade in the sun, and hid from the mind the perception of things dear to him. Thinking of his parents still brought tears to his eyes. In their absence he had to fend for himself and as he realised this, his resolve to seek vengeance on his uncles grew all the stronger.

He was out on the farm early one morning when he saw his grandmother milking the cows. It was generally considered a woman's job to do the milking and so it was something she did, striking out with her milk pail regularly twice a day. The two cows were tethered so that they wouldn't wander off and graze on the crops or stray onto other people's land, for there were no fences on the farm. A plan began to form in his head. What if he untethered the cows and let them roam free? His uncles were supposed to be responsible for them and when the cows were gone, they would take the blame. It was an easy thing to do. All that was necessary was to untie the ropes from the stakes and let them go. He could think of no other way of venting his dislike for his uncles which would avoid him being involved. He waited until his grandmother had finished milking, made sure no-one else was around to see him, then untied the tethers. The cows continued grazing, unaware they were free to wander wherever they wanted. Having done the deed, Winstone returned to his house with a feeling of satisfaction, got out pencils and paper, started drawing and awaited the outcome of his deed. At midday he went over to his grandmother's house for some maize-meal and a drink of milk. Nobody seemed to have noticed the absence of the cows. After the meal he returned to his sketching.

Late that afternoon Martha went out for the second milking of the day. It was then she discovered the cows had gone. In a panic she shouted to Elias.

'Elias, come quick. Who's moved the cows? Where have they gone?' Then she noticed the stakes were there without the tethers. When Elias came hurrying up to her, she said, 'look the tethers have gone as well as the cows. Somebody must have untied them. They were firmly tied when I last milked them.'

'Well, who could have done that?' There was a look of consternation on Elias's face. Cows were valuable, so were his crops and what is more, he would be in trouble if they had strayed onto neighbouring land. He might have to pay compensation. 'I can't remember this happening before. You don't think it's those twins up to their tricks again? You don't think they have done this so the blame can rest on young Winstone do you?'

'I wouldn't put it past them,' observed Martha dryly. 'I expect the twins will be eating their meal by now. We had better go and see whether we can find those animals. Goodness knows how long they've been away.'

They searched their land without success. Neither could they see them on neighbouring land.

'I hope nobody has stolen them,' Elias remarked in desperation. 'It'll be a great loss to us if they've been taken. I'll shall have to go and talk to Matthew and Mark. They must know something about this,' he said with an air of resignation. 'I'm sure it's going to lead to trouble.'

There was nobody at Mark's home. They must be at Matthew's. He banged on the door.

'Come in', someone shouted. He opened the door and stood on the threshold.

'Where have the cows gone?' he demanded.

'What do you mean, Dad?' asked Matthew in surprise.

'The cows have gone. They're nowhere to be seen. Didn't you notice?'

'Well, they were grazing happily this morning,' said Mark.

'Come on. Don't mess with me. Where have you put them?'

'We haven't put them anywhere, Dad, honest,' Matthew replied.

The twins are on the defensive Elias thought. Just like they were when Delia disappeared.

'I don't believe you. You've hidden those animals so that Winstone can take the blame, just like you did with his shirt and schoolbooks. Now come on, where have you put them?'

'You never believe us, do you, Dad?' complained Mathew.

'Is it any wonder? When something goes wrong, you always deny it's your fault. Those cows are valuable, and they're your responsibility and you don't bother looking after them. Why haven't you done so? Once again you've been acting irresponsibly.'

At that moment someone was coming up the farm track shouting for Elias. Barnabas, their neighbour came into view leading two cows, their cows. Barnabas was a good friend with a great sense of humour. He had helped out Elias on many occasions when he was in difficulty.

'See here, I found these two ladies grazing on the side of the track. Wandering all over the place they were. It's a good thing there was no traffic about. In this half-light they could easily have been run into, especially on a bend. If you let them graze out there you ought to put lights on them,' he chuckled.

On this particular occasion Elias didn't appreciate his neighbour's teasing. It nettled him, made him feel incompetent. 'That's good of you to round them up Barnabas. I am much obliged to you. Thank you for bringing them in.'

'They must have slipped their tethers,' Barnabas observed.

'I have a suspicion someone helped them do it.' Elias half glanced at the twins. 'They were certainly firmly tethered earlier in the day. I hope they didn't get on your land.'

'There's no sign of that. Anyway, I'm glad they're safely home,' and with a wave of the hand he was gone.

'Honest, Dad, we had nothing to do with this,' said Matthew as they were tethering the cows again.

'Then who could have done it?'

'I can only think of Winstone. It wouldn't be difficult for him to untie the knots.'

'Winstone? Why would he do it?'

Matthew shrugged his shoulders. 'Boredom I suppose. He sits a long time alone in that house of his, poor kid. Perhaps he needed a bit of entertainment.'

That remark smacked of criticism. Elias was aware Winstone was left too much on his own and he knew he ought to do something about it.

'Come on, you'd better go over to the house. I'll go and get Winstone.'

Martha lit the lamp. Winstone arrived with a puzzled look on his face. Why had he been summoned when the blame was surely on the shoulders of Mark and Matthew?

'Tell me,' said Elias, addressing Winstone, 'who untied the cattle today?'

He hadn't expected to be asked that question. Grandfather's tone of voice was serious.

'I don't know,' said Winstone speaking slowly. He was looking at his feet.

'They were tied up when Grandmother went to milk them this morning. I saw her milking them.'

'And what did you do after that?'

Winstone hesitated. 'I... I went back and did some drawings.'

'No, you didn't. You waited until Grandmother had finished milking and then you untied them.'

Winstone was astonished. How did Grandfather know that? He was sure he wasn't around at the time. Winstone continued to look at his feet. He said nothing.

'Well answer me,' said Elias in a very firm voice. Winstone remained silent. 'You did it didn't you?' Tears were rolling down Winstone's face. 'Why did you do it?'

Between sobs he said, 'It's my uncles. They're always teasing me. Why can't they leave me alone? I hate them. I never feel safe when they're around. The only safe place is my home. I wanted to punish them. I thought if I untied the cows, they would get the blame for it. I didn't think I'd get the blame.'

The twins stood in the room and remained silent. Elias felt sorry for his grandson. He understood his motive. He could understand he was frustrated by his uncles. He was convinced his grandson would not have misbehaved in this way had it not been for the twins. Nevertheless, he had told a lie to his grandfather and he had endangered two valuable animals. In Elias's tenet he had to be punished.

'You lied to me and you've risked the lives of those animals. They were found out on the track you know. People drive along there fast. They could've been killed. You have to be punished for such bad behaviour. You're seven years old next week and you ought to know better. I shall beat you seven times with my cane so that you will remember this occasion.' He reached for his cane, the same cane that had chastened Matthew and Mark when they had been young. Although it had been used on Winstone once before, it was the first time the twins saw it used on another member of the family. Its use brought to mind a long catalogue of their misdeeds.

'Don't be too hard on him,' warned Martha in a moment of sympathy.

In Elias's eyes the use of the cane was more a token of punishment than it was an instrument of torment. He was appalled at the violence some neighbours meted out when they beat their wives. He believed beating a wife was the negation of love for one who should be regarded as an equal. Furthermore, beating a child should never ever be done in anger. Inflicting vicious pain destroyed the child's self-esteem and belittled the adult using the instrument of chastisement. All that was needed was a light touch. The act of bending over and being caned was enough to shame a child and shame, he believed, was more effective than pain.

When he had finished caning Winstone, Elias turned to Martha and said, 'go across and put him to bed. He will go without his meal this evening.'

As she put him to bed Winstone sobbed, 'please forgive me Grandmother, please, please forgive me.'

'You've had your punishment. It's all over now. I forgive you,' she said in her usual matter of fact voice. But it brought him little comfort. There were no loving words which Winstone was desperate to hear and no kiss to comfort him.

Meanwhile, back at the house Elias was lambasting the twins.

'That boy has been punished unnecessarily. It's all your fault. Your treatment of him is disgraceful. You make his life a misery with your teasing. You heard him say he hates you for it. What a sad observation from a young boy who should have a feeling of love for his uncles. As grown men you should know better. You criticise him for spending so much time in his home but it's you who drive him there. If you were decent individuals you would spend time with him, encouraging him, playing games with him, not tormenting him. I just don't understand your mentality. I'm ashamed of you. Now go, get out of my sight,' he shouted, pointing at the door.

At the age of seven Winstone had a great deal of independence and considerable maturity for a child of his age. He had lost the chubbiness of his earlier years and was good looking. He had inherited his mother's smile and his father's twinkly eyes. At one time a pensive and sometimes solemn child as the result of spending long hours on his own before he was old enough to go to school, he was growing in self -confidence. He bathed himself regularly in the little corrugated iron enclosure that served as a bathroom. Squatting over a bowl of warm water he had heated on his kitchen fire, he scooped the water over his naked body with his hands, soaped himself, scooped more water over to rinse himself, then stood for five or six minutes to dry in the sun. It was delicious to feel the warmth beating down on his front and then, turning around to dry his back. Martha still cut his thick curly black hair to within a quarter of an inch of his scalp, but he cleaned his teeth himself and rubbed off the dried, dead skin around his feet from walking barefoot with pumice.

When he first started school, Elias said he was old enough to work regularly on the farm. In the morning he would go across to his grandparents to take tea then set about doing an hour's weeding before going to school. As the twins were late risers, Winstone was never disturbed by them. When he became older and it was the school holidays, he was obliged to work on the farm every morning except Sundays. The rest of the day he was free to do what he liked. Then he could meet up with his school friends either on the farm or at one of their homes, and when he wanted to, he could return home, get out his pencils, crayons and paints and draw pictures to his heart's content.

He didn't find work on the farm a chore because he loved being on the land. It gave him pleasure to feel the rich warm earth on his hands and between his toes and to see the first green shoots appearing from the seeds he had sown. It was a wonder to him how life sprang out of such a small, dead looking object to grow into a tall plant; how something as small as a seed could grow to feed a whole family. Here the land was blessed with good fertile soil and regular rainfall. There were other parts of the country where the climate was fickle, if not hostile and through lack of rain the crops withered and people starved. Yet there were many even in this fertile area who lacked food, either because they had no land to cultivate or were too poor to buy the seeds they needed to grow their own food. Poverty there always was, but abject poverty was something Winstone had not known about until he started school. Nobody should be allowed to go hungry, he thought. 'If I were to own this land, I would work hard to grow enough to give away to the poor and needy.'

Whereas Elias regarded Winstone as a nuisance on the farm when he was young, he now saw him as a capable worker and one who was able to take on some of his own workload. The age gap and the animosity between Winstone and the twins was such that they could never have worked together. Elias therefore made sure he allocated tasks that ensured they were kept apart. It was a good policy. Winstone was enthusiastic. He worked fast and competently and had the twins been with him they would simply have slackened off and left most of the work to him.

CHAPTER FIVE

'Grandfather,' said Winstone one day when he came home from school, 'I want to have a serious talk with you. Can we go and sit on the bench outside?'

Elias and Martha were sitting resting in their favourite chairs in the living room. Elias looked up from the letter he was reading. He could see that something was troubling his grandson. He thought it must be something personal that Winstone didn't want Martha to hear. He put the letter down, walked into the yard and the two of them settled down on the bench in the warm sun of late afternoon.

'What is it?' Elias asked.

'Grandfather,' Winstone began. 'What was it like when you were at school?'

'That was a long time ago. Things were quite different when I was young. There weren't many schools about then. Your Grandmother and I were lucky, because there was a school near where we lived run by the missionaries. It wasn't free but at the same time it wasn't expensive. In the beginning our parents could afford to send us there. We were there for four years, then the missionaries put up the fees and we had to leave. We were sad. We were both clever. I thought with a good education and if I married your grandmother, I could get a good job and we could work our way out of poverty. That wasn't to be. We had no qualifications and I had no opportunity to get a good job in those days.

When my father died, I took over farming his land. I worked hard. We saved and saved and managed to buy more land and we saved enough to send your uncles and aunt to school. But because we had so little money I've never travelled away from this area. They say that Kenya is a big country and that there's a big capital city. Your uncle John has been there several times on business. He says there are huge buildings of concrete and glass and roads with hard surfaces. It's difficult to imagine. He's tried to persuade me to visit his home in Eldoret several times, but I've said "no". I don't like it in his car when he drives fast. It's dangerous and it unsettles me.'

'Did you get punished in school if you didn't pass your exams?'

Elias thought for a moment. 'No, I don't think so. You see, because we did well at school and passed our exams we never had to be punished.'

'They punish us at our school,' Winstone said.

'Yes, I know they do. I am not really in favour of it. I believe if a child fails exams it should be given encouragement not punishment. Punishment achieves nothing. But you don't get punished. You always get good results, don't you?'

'Yes, but other boys get punished and girls as well. You know, Grandfather, a terrible thing happened today. You know my friend Absalom, don't you - the one I gave a pencil and writing paper to when we first started school? He never seems to pass his exams and he gets punished every time. Today the teacher made him run four times round the playing field as punishment and he collapsed on the ground. He must have fainted or something. We rushed over to him and he was unconscious when we carried him back to the classroom. His face was white. I thought he had died!'

Elias saw tears welling up in his eyes. He could see the boy was upset. He put his hand on Winstone's knee to comfort him. 'What happened then Wanyonyi?' he asked.

Winstone swallowed hard and fought back the tears. 'They laid him down and put a blanket over him and eventually he came around. After a bit they sat him up and gave him some food and a drink. I was so relieved he was alive. I held his hand for a while to let him know I was concerned for him. I was furious with that teacher. I told him he was a cruel man to punish Absalom just for failing an exam. I thought I would get the cane but instead he just turned away from me. I think he felt ashamed.

By the time school finished, Absalom was able to stand again but he was very weak. Seth and Hillary and I said we would walk home with him since Absalom refused to have a teacher go with him. We walked slowly. He was unsteady on his feet. Every now and then we had to stop while he sat and rested. When we reached the stepping- stones we walked through the water and held his hands so that he didn't slip on the stones. When Hillary and Seth stopped at their homes, I went all the way back with Absalom.

You know, we often play at each other's places, but we have never been to Absalom's place and now I know why. He told me about his home. His mother sells old clothes in the market, but she doesn't make much money because they are very worn. His father is an alcoholic and doesn't have a job. He takes most of the money his wife earns. So, there is little to buy food with. He said he always goes hungry. They don't even drink tea. They just drink hot water. Often, they can't afford paraffin for their lamp, so they just go to bed when it gets dark. Absalom says that's why he fails his exams because he has no light to do his homework or read the textbooks when it's his turn to have them. And then he gets punished for it! It's just not fair.

When we got to his home, his mother was not there. She was still at the market. I asked where his little sister was. He said she would be either with her mother or visiting an aunt. She liked going to the aunt because she was given food there. I sat with him for a time while he rested. The place was pretty awful. There were two little huts with thatched roofs and a kitchen, but the thatch was old and let in the rain. He said his dad was going to re-thatch them, but he never got around to doing it. Also, there was almost no furniture.'

'I know about that family,' Elias said. 'There are nine children altogether. Your friend and his sister were born sometime after the other seven. The older ones all left home because the conditions got so bad after their father turned to drink. Some got jobs elsewhere and others married early. That poor mother has had a bad time. As far as I know, none of them help to support her. It must be a miserable life.'

'Grandfather, Absalom doesn't get enough to eat. Cassava is what they eat most of the time and that's not nourishing. We have plenty of food here. Can't Absalom come and live here? He can share my house and I can cook food for him in my kitchen so that Grandmother doesn't have to provide for him, and we can do our homework together in the evening and he will learn his lessons properly.'

Elias was a cautious man. He never made rash decisions. He was certainly not going to be rushed into the prospect of having a stranger living on the farm. He needed to chew it over in his mind before he made a decision.

'I'll give it some thought,' he said. 'I know nothing about that boy except what you told me. I don't know how well behaved he is or how trustworthy. There are many rascals and no-gooders around here you know. Besides I don't know what his mother would think of such a proposal nor indeed his father for that matter.'

Winstone knew from experience it would be some days before his grandfather made up his mind. At least he felt relieved that he had the courage to speak about what was foremost in his thoughts, but he was still worried for Absalom. Absalom was so weak from lack of food that unless something was done quickly, he was going to become really ill and miss school altogether.

That evening, sitting alone in his house a thought came to him: Absalom's mother sold old clothes in the market. She didn't make much money because they were so worn. In the wardrobe there were three dresses belonging to his mother. They were almost new, and they were pretty. Winstone hadn't seen anybody else wearing such lovely dresses. What if he took one to Absalom's mother to sell on her stall? There were no other clothes like it in the market. It seemed to him any one of them would fetch a good price - enough he hoped to buy at least a week's supply of nourishing food. But which of the three should he choose? And was it right he should give away something that wasn't his? What would Mama have said if she had been around? What would his grandparents think if they found out one dress was missing? Dare he part with something that to him was one of the last links with his memory of his mother? He tussled with these thoughts. They buzzed around his head like a swarm of flies. He was not used to making such a weighty decision. He felt bereft of someone to advise him. It seemed to him on the one hand he had the means of helping people in need but on the other he might be betraying his mother. That night when he went to bed, he prayed to God to tell him what to do. After all, if Mama was with God, she could tell him what her son should do.

When he awoke in the morning Winstone felt convinced he should go ahead with his plan. When he arrived home after school, he opened the wardrobe door. He still had one final decision to make. Which of the three dresses should he choose to give away? Two of them had intricate small patterns on them. On the third the patterns were bold and in strident colours. He considered that one would stand out better in the marketplace and attract more customers than the other two. He took the dress off its hanger and laid it on his bed. He wasn't sure how to fold it. After several attempts he managed to fold the sleeves across the bodice and then from the hem upwards, folded the dress over and over until it fitted into a paper bag he had. Then he set off for Absalom's house.

When he arrived, he found the mother sitting by the door of one of the huts. Nobody else was around. Her head was bowed. She looked tired after a long day at the market. Hearing his footsteps, she looked up at Winstone in surprise. Winstone thought he should be polite and greet her as an adult would have done. '*Mulembe* Mama Absalom,' he said and shook hands, his left hand clutching his right arm as a sign of respect.

'Where have you come from?' she asked. 'I don't recognise you.'

Winstone explained he was Absalom's friend. 'I came to bring you something,' he said, and handed over the bag.

'Whatever is this?' she said, opening the bag and peering inside. 'Wherever did this come from?' Her voice gave away her curiosity.

'It's one of my mother's dresses. I thought you could sell it on your stall.'

'Does your mother know about this?' she asked him.

'My mother is dead.'

'No! I knew your father died. I attended his funeral but when did your mother die? Was it long after your father? News goes around this community very quickly, so I'm surprised I didn't know. When was your mother's funeral? I never heard about it.'

'There was no funeral. My mother died away from home.'

'But there should still have been a funeral,' she insisted.

'No, she went away before she died, and we didn't know where she had gone.'

'Then how do you know she is dead?'

'My grandparents said so.'

The woman shook her head in disbelief. 'So, you are an orphan then. Why have you brought me this dress?' She looked at him quizzically. 'It's a beautiful piece of work. More beautiful than you find around here.'

'It's because of Absalom. I was so shocked at what happened yesterday. He doesn't get enough food and if he isn't given more, he will never be well enough to go back to school. He said you haven't much money. I thought if I brought you this dress you could sell it at the market and use the money to buy more food.'

'My dear child, I was so grateful for what you did for Absalom yesterday. You really are a good friend. I'm surprised one of the teachers didn't arrange to bring him home. It is a pity he is not here now. He's gone to collect firewood. He was too weak to go to school. He stayed in bed most of the day. You're right, his health is failing through lack of food. You see, I'm ashamed to say it, but my husband is an alcoholic and drinks all our money away. He's one of those that goes to the drying shed and drinks with your uncles.'

She turned her attention to the dress again, standing up and holding it at full length. 'It's beautiful fabric and the dress is such a lovely design. I wish I was young and slim again. I would love to wear it!' Then she turned to Winstone and, putting her arm round him, exclaimed, 'Oh, my son, my son, you have done us such a good turn. I can't thank you enough.'

For a moment Winstone was stunned. "My son, my son," filled him with alarm. "My son, my son," was something Mama used to say to him before she disappeared. Now this woman was saying the same thing! But he was not her son. Was this some kind of portent? He felt a shiver glance through his body. Then it dawned on him she was probably saying it merely as an expression of endearment.

'You know where my tarpaulin is don't you?' she continued, 'where I lay out all my clothes in the market. It's under one of those big trees. I've got a clothes hanger. I shall hang this dress from one of the branches. Everybody will see it. They will wonder where it came from. I'm sure it will sell very easily!

CHAPTER SIX

'I don't know why you can't make up your mind about that boy, Absalom,' Martha said to Elias. 'It's been five days now since Winstone asked you. He's waited patiently. He certainly has self-discipline. He doesn't pester people like some young ones do, but he must be thinking you've forgotten about him.'

They had just finished a meal. Winstone had left the room and gone out to meet his friends. Elias sat thinking, elbows on the table, head in his hands. He was considering the pros and cons of Winstone's request.

'No, I haven't forgotten him. I've just been turning things over in my mind. It's just that we don't know much about that kid. He's obviously a weakling but that's probably down to lack of food. We certainly don't want to look after a sick child. Nor do we know anything about his moral standards. With his father continually drunk that boy can't have had much discipline drilled into him. For instance, is he trustworthy? Would he steal like some kids around here do? If he comes here, do we have to clothe him as well as feed him? Also, we have to take the twins into account. They behave abominably to Winstone. How do you think they would treat this boy? We could be taking on a lot of responsibility you know. And we don't even know whether his mother would agree to such a plan let alone his father. She probably relies on her son to do the chores. I can't think that useless husband does much for her. Besides we don't even know whether the boy would want to come here.'

'Well let's look at the positive side of things,' said Martha. 'It would do Winstone good to have a companion. It's not right for a young boy to spend so much time by himself. Secondly, I can't imagine Absalom's family circumstances will change much unless - glory be - his father gives up drinking. Personally, I think he's too far gone to do that. So how is that boy going to survive if he isn't fed properly? Thirdly, Winstone tells me they can't afford paraffin, so the boy can't do his homework at night. If he was here the two of them could study together and he might then pass some of his exams, unless malnutrition has gone so far as to affect his mental ability. Fourthly, I don't think the twins would pose any problem. And if they are thick with the boy's father, they're not going to upset him by fooling around with his son. Fifthly, Winstone has to work on the farm before he goes to school and for half a day in the holidays. The same would have to apply to the boy in return for staying with us once he has regular meals and is well enough to work, and with an extra pair of hands in the fields that would take some of the pressure off you.'

Elias smiled inwardly. Martha had a wonderful way with her, always positive, always seeing the bright side of things and always persuasive. Yes, she could be strong-minded, demanding and at times unloving. Yet she had wisdom and the foresight which he lacked. He on the other hand was tolerant, warm, and forgiving. Their dispositions complemented each other, and in many ways, they were perfectly matched.

'I think you should tell Winstone you will go and talk to Absalom's mother and ask her what she thinks about his proposition,' Martha continued. 'Mind you, you will also have to remind him that Absalom's father has to agree as well and that might be difficult if his drinking makes him uncooperative. I doubt Winstone has said anything to the boy about his plan before you have given him an answer. So, you must make it clear to Winstone that his friend might not want to come and live here.'

Elias brightened a little. Life for that young lad must be pretty rotten for him. He wondered what he was really like. He'd only seen him in passing when Winstone had brought his friends round to play. The boy was still young. Given regular food he could yet grow strong, and if he was prepared to work, the prospect of another hand on the farm could be a blessing.

'Alright then, but if that boy works on the farm with Winstone I shall have to make sure I allocate jobs for them that will keep them well away from the twins. If I'm not around when Winstone comes back, tell him I want to see him when I return. Rather than go around to the boy's home I think I'll talk to his mother when I go to the market tomorrow. It's better that way. We can talk openly and won't be hampered by other family members.'

That evening Elias told Winstone what he planned to do. 'Have you said anything to the boy about coming here?' he asked Winstone.

Winstone said no he hadn't because he was waiting for his grandfather to make up his mind.

'In any case,' said Winstone, 'Absalom hasn't been at school. I haven't seen him since the day I walked him home. I guess he's still pretty weak.'

The next day Absalom did return to school. As soon as he saw Winstone he went up and thanked him.

'You know, my mother was in tears when she got home. She was so upset she had no means of feeding us proper food. She said she believed she was a hopeless mother. When my father came home in the evening drunk, she demanded money from him but he wouldn't give it. They had an argument and it turned into a fight. My little sister was terrified. I tried to separate them. In the end my father threw down a few coins, but it was too late in the evening to buy any food. All we had left was a little maize-meal. It didn't come to much shared between us. Normally I have difficulty sleeping when I'm hungry, but I guess I was drained from the day's events. I slept until after I should have left for school. When I got up, I felt so weak I had to go to bed again and it wasn't until just before you came with that dress that I felt well enough to get some firewood.

My mother sold that dress the same day she took it to market. A lot of bargaining went on. The woman who bought it tried hard to knock down the price. She haggled for a long time, walked away, came back and haggled again. She was a visitor to Cheptais from a large town somewhere. My mother could see from the clothes she wore that she was well off. So, she stuck her ground and eventually the woman paid up. We've eaten so well since then and I feel a lot better thanks to you. You're a really good guy. Of course, my mum was worried about keeping her earnings safe. So, she got me to dig a hole in the ground marked by a stick to bury some of the money so that my father doesn't get his hands on it. If he had done, it would all be used for drink.'

It was a difficult day at school for Winstone. He badly wanted to tell Absalom what he had talked about to his grandfather. He was desperate to know whether or not he would be willing to live on the farm. At the same time, he couldn't stop thinking about Grandfather and the conversation he was having with Absalom's mother. How would she react? Would she say "no" because she needed Absalom's support at home more than what might be a better life for him? Could she give no answer because she didn't know how her husband would react? Or was she against the idea altogether? He was so occupied with his thoughts in one of the lessons the teacher had to call out his name three times before he realised he was being spoken too. The children in the class turned and stared at him. They thought he had suddenly gone deaf.

'So, you gave away one of your mother's dresses,' Elias said when Winstone came home from school. Winstone froze. He hadn't wanted his grandparents to know what he had done. He hung his head and said nothing. Martha came into the room. She had heard what Elias had said.

'You didn't tell us because I suppose you were worried what we would say.'

Winstone nodded his head.

'Well,' she continued, 'I think you did a very generous thing.'

Winstone looked at his grandmother with a feeling of relief.

'That poor woman must have been at her wits end. No money and her son in desperate need of food. That was very thoughtful of you, and generous too. I'm proud of you.'

That was praise indeed, coming from his grandmother.

'I was worried because I didn't know whether I had the right to part with Mama's dress and I didn't know how she would have felt about it if she was still alive.'

'I think she would have approved of what you did,' said Elias. 'That woman was so grateful to you. She said she was impressed by the way you greeted her and shook hands. She told me she thought you were fine young man!'

Nobody had spoken to Winstone in those terms before. He felt a warm glow of pride inside but he was too modest to let it show.

'Now I expect you're wondering what Absalom's mother said. She said it would be one less mouth to feed and that would make life easier for her. She also said that the little one will be looked after by her aunt on school days until Absalom comes home from school. Then she wants Absalom to collect her and take her home and sit with his sister and do one or two household chores until she gets back from the market. Then he will come to us. She also said that since both of you are nearly nine you should be quite capable of looking after yourselves.'

'What about her husband?' asked Winstone. 'What does she think he will say?'

'She said her husband has never been interested in the family. He gave the older children no support; that's why they left home. She doesn't think he'll be the slightest bothered if Absalom comes to live with us.'

'That's great!' said Winstone enthusiastically. 'So, what do we do now, Grandfather?'

'We have to wait. Absalom will be told about your plan when his mother gets home this evening. She warned me: she's not at all sure he'll want to leave home and live here.'

Winstone didn't have much to say at mealtime. One hurdle had been overcome but the other was more problematic. What if Absalom decided he didn't want to leave home? What a blow that would be! He and Absalom were really good friends and had been ever since they began school. They seemed to get on so well together. If Absalom rejected the idea, Winstone knew he himself would feel rebuffed and with those feelings, the friendship would probably wither and he didn't want that to happen. He wished he didn't have to go to school the next day for fear of being rejected. Absalom would surely have made up his mind by then.

As it happened, he didn't have to worry. Winstone was just finishing the last of his homework when someone was thumping the door hard. Before he could open it, Absalom burst in. He had run all the way and was out of breath.

'So,' he said, between gasps, 'so this is going to be my new home. I'm coming here to live! It's great! It's really great! I can't believe it.'

Next moment they were hugging each other. Despite the hard times he had endured, Absalom was a bright eyed, alert, smiling individual with more than his fair share of self-confidence. His legs and arms were spindly, and in contrast with his lean face, he sported a bush of black curly hair which his mother cut infrequently. Small in stature for his age and thin, probably through malnutrition, Winstone could feel the bones in his body while he hugged him.

'When can I come?' Absalom demanded in his invariably enthusiastic manner.

Winstone was taken aback by the sudden turn of events.

'I... I don't know,' he stammered. 'We'll have to ask Grandfather. I don't know what he has planned.'

'Are you sure you don't mind me coming to live with you? You're used to being on your own. It'll be different with another person in the house.'

'No, no,' said Winstone, anxious to convey to Absalom that he was really pleased to be sharing the house with him. 'Actually, I've been lonely here. I couldn't have wished for anything better. We'll have to make a few rearrangements though. For instance, do we sleep in different bedrooms or in the same bedroom?'

'In the same bedroom of course. We sleep together.'

'Then we'll have to bring my father's old bed into my room. You don't mind sleeping in a dead man's bed?'

'No, of course not,' said Absalom. 'Why should I? We've all got to die sometime! Just imagine if nobody slept in beds people had died in. There would be a mountain of unused beds lying about everywhere!'

They laughed. It was going to be fun being together.

'Can you cook?' asked Winstone.

'Chapattis and maize meal, that's all. We never eat chicken or meat. It's too expensive and we don't buy vegetables except for cassava.'

'Sometimes we'll eat here and sometimes with my grandparents,' said Winstone. 'We can cook in my kitchen. We can make tea in the morning before school. In the evening you can do the maize-meal and I'll cook the vegetables. Grandfather says people need to eat vegetables to keep healthy.

'Shall we do our own washing?' asked Absalom. 'I don't see why not. Mama has an iron. We could even try using that.'

Winstone was longing to tell him something. 'Turn around. Have you seen yourself from behind?'

Absalom looked surprised. 'How can I see myself from behind?'

'You can't but I can,' said Winstone. 'There's a tear in your shorts and a bit of bum is showing.'

'I know. Mum said she would mend it, but she has never had time.' Then with a cheeky grin Absalom said, 'I don't mind really, 'cos it attracts a lot of girls!'

They laughed again. There was a knock at the door. It was Elias.

'I thought I heard voices,' he said addressing Winstone. 'It's getting late you know.'

'I know it's late, but Absalom is here. This is Absalom, Grandfather. He was so excited at the thought of living here he couldn't wait to tell me at school tomorrow. Absalom, this is my grandfather.' They shook hands. 'We've just been planning things Grandfather. I'm really pleased to have a friend staying with me. We're going to be great company for each other.'

Elias turned to Absalom. 'Welcome to our farm,' he said. 'I'm glad you've made this decision. I think it's probably the right thing for you both, but do you understand the terms your mother and I came to? You're to look after your sister before your mother comes home from market and you're to help Winstone on the farm in the mornings before school when you're fit enough. You'll be fed well here, and I think you'll soon get your strength back.'

Absalom said he understood and looked forward to helping Winstone on the land.

'Now it's time you went home, Absalom,' Elias said. 'You can find your way in the dark I suppose?' Absalom nodded. 'And it's bedtime for you, Winstone.'

That night Winstone did not sleep much. He was thrilled at the thought that his best friend was going to stay with him. He had been lonely as an only child. Now he was going to have a companion of his own age he could confide in, one with whom he could share the joys and disappointments of life. Together they could overcome the lack in their lives, the one of food and the other of companionship.

CHAPTER SEVEN

Elias was right. His plan to separate the boys and the twins while working on the land turned out well. The twins kept their distance and did not trouble the boys out of respect for Absalom's father. The exceptions were when Matthew and Mark had been out all night and came home roaring drunk.

Later in life, when he was middle-aged, Winstone remembered one particular occasion when the drunkards had returned from a night out at the old drying barn in a state of inebriation. It was a Friday morning and a day of exams. He and Absalom had finished their morning chores and were gathering cow dung for spreading on the school floor. They had just come out of the byre when their paths crossed with the drunkards. In a state of riotous hilarity and smelling strongly of alcohol the twins chased them. Winstone had tripped and fallen in Matthew's path who, unsteady on his feet, fell on top of him. Thinking this was fun, Mark had then run at Absalom and they too landed on the ground. Neither twin was capable of getting to their feet again but when Winstone and Absalom had extricated themselves they realised they were in a real mess. Dung and mud clung to their uniforms. In a state of distress, they had tried to scrape off as much as they could then had gone to the well, drawn water and tried to wash away what stains they could. By now they were late for lessons. The sun was hot, and they reckoned their clothes would be reasonably dry by the time they reached school. They had been summoned to the headmaster's office. The cane was lying ominously on his desk.

'Why are you late for school this morning?' the headmaster had demanded. 'The exams have already started. Why are your uniforms filthy dirty and why haven't you brought in any dung to school?'

They explained what had happened and were expecting the cane. But instead of picking up the cane the headmaster told them to remove their shirts to lessen the smell in his office, pointed to a table and told them to sit. He then fetched an exam paper for each of them and they sat the exam in his office under his watchful eye.

They had to put their shirts on again in the lunch break. Their classmates had teased them remorselessly for their odorous garments. When school finished the headmaster handed Winstone a letter addressed to his grandfather. Elias read it, then left the house for a long time. Whether it was to placate his anguish or to berate the twins Winstone never knew, but when his grandfather returned, he sat silent for much of the evening.

Thinking of those days, Winstone realised what a strain life had been for his grandparents. Farming was very much a family affair. It required everybody in the household to help with the ploughing, the sowing, the weeding and the harvesting, whether it was fruit or sugar cane, coffee beans, sweet potatoes, cabbage or all the other crops they grew. With only two incompetent and uncooperative sons and two young boys, much of the work had fallen on Elias's shoulders and Martha had been obliged to work in the fields and look after the cows as and when she could. As a consequence, the land had not been used to its full potential. There was simply not enough manpower to manage it efficiently.

It was not difficult for Absalom to move in with Winstone. He had practically nothing to bring. He arrived after school wearing his school uniform. His other clothing consisted of an old sweater and an anorak from his mother's stall, a pair of flip-flops and a spare shirt and spare shorts, which, like his school trousers, were in need of repair. He possessed no underpants. He carried with him a toothbrush and his one proud possession, a sheath knife. Like everyone else, he slept in his day clothes. Winstone had blankets enough left over from his parents for Absalom to use so he was at least warm in bed. Winstone was impressed with the sheath knife.

'Where did you get this from?' he asked, taking the knife out of its sheath and examining its shiny blade. The sheath was made of leather. The leather had patterns burnt into it and was embossed with an animal that looked like an antelope but clearly wasn't. Attached to the sheath was a piece of leather with a hole in it which fitted over a knob at the end of the knife handle to prevent the knife from coming out of its sheath. On the blade was engraved "Brusletto" with a star beneath it. The handle had a metal core with what looked like leather binding in the middle and the end of the handle curved underneath to give a grip for the little finger. 'I really like it,' he remarked. 'It's a proper knife.'

'An uncle gave it to me before he died,' Absalom said. 'He got it when he was serving in the army somewhere in Europe. He said that every boy needs a knife in life. Funny isn't it? It rhymes: a knife in life.'

'What do you use it for?'

'I whittle with it,' said Absalom.

'What does "whittle" mean?'

'It means cutting pieces of wood bit by bit to make something,' said Absalom.

Winstone was intrigued. 'What do you make then?'

'Well, I usually make little people. Look I'll show you.' He took a piece of wood from his trouser pocket and began to shape it, paring it with his knife piece by piece until there was a small pile of shavings on the floor. First a head appeared, then the body shaped in such a way as to create arms and finally cutting away to make legs.

'I could never do that. I can draw a body, but I can't make a figure.'

'I bet you could,' said Absalom. 'Here's another piece of wood. Go on, try.'

Winstone's attempt at carving was not a success. He did not have the dexterity that Absalom had to hold the wood and pare pieces off it. The knife kept slipping. The piece of wood got smaller and smaller until there was almost no figure left at all. Absalom made fun of him for being so incapable.

'Alright,' said Winstone defiantly, 'then I'm going to get a pencil and drawing pad and I want you to draw a figure.'

Try as he might, Absalom was unable to draw a reasonable looking figure. He broke the pencil lead twice and Winstone had to re-sharpen it.

'I can't do it. I need something hard to press on, not a flimsy bit of pencil,' Absalom complained, putting down the pencil and getting up from the table.

'Okay,' conceded Winstone. 'I'll stick to drawing and you stick to whittling. We'll make a good pair. I can draw the figure and you can copy it in wood.'

Having Absalom living with him brought an extra dimension to Winstone's life. Since Absalom had to be at home looking after his little sister Ellen each school day, Winstone naturally became involved with Absalom's family. His mother was worried about the condition of the roofs of their two little huts. The thatch was old and as the weeks went by more and more water leaked inside when it rained.

'I wish we could do something about it,' Absalom said. 'All their clothes and the beds are getting wet and I don't know how to repair a roof.'

'I'll ask Grandfather,' volunteered Winstone. 'He used to live in a thatched hut before he built his new house. Sometimes he says he wishes he still had thatch because it has better insulation against the sun than corrugated iron and the house doesn't get so hot in the daytime and anyway it is much quieter when it rains. But he says it's not easy to thatch a building that is round.'

When Winstone asked him, Elias said it was getting more difficult to find grass for thatching because as the population grew the type of grass used for thatching was ploughed up and replaced by grass for grazing. However, he knew a place where thatching grass still grew. He would take the boys there but they would have to harvest it themselves. He would also show them how to thatch but they would have to learn to do it themselves. He did not have the time to help them himself.

The boys enjoyed cutting the grass using Elias's tools. It was tied into bundles and carried back to Absalom's home. It surprised them how heavy the bundles were.

They made a crude ladder out of wood they had cut from a tree, so they could reach the top of the roofs.

Elias came over and laid the first bundle of thatch to show the boys how it was done. When the work was completed, the clean new thatch made the huts look very smart. Absalom's mother said it was almost like having a new home.

Towards the end of the year another problem arose. Ellen was to start school in the new year but there was no money to buy a school uniform. She needed not only a blouse and a skirt. All girls had to wear nickers too whereas boys were not required to wear underpants, the emphasis being on clean necks, faces, hands and uniforms, teachers inspected girls' nickers for cleanliness on a regular basis. It was then that Winstone had a good idea.

'Why don't we have a stall in the market?'

Absalom wondered what they could sell.

'Easy,' said Winstone. 'Can you whittle animals?'

'I think I can.'

'Good. I'll draw some animals - no, I'll paint some and you can whittle some. We can sell matching pictures and animals. I've never tried but it might be possible to use my water colour paints on the animals' bodies, so they look more life-like. You can make some dolls as well if you like. If Grandmother can find some bits of cloth for us and lets me use a needle and some of her thread, we can make trousers for the boy dolls and skirts for the girls. How about that?'

'Brilliant idea.' Absalom was enthusiastic. 'We could do it on Saturday and Sunday evenings after dark when we don't have homework to do.'

They enjoyed those evenings sitting together round the hurricane lamp. They turned up the wick as far as they could without it smoking. The heat it gave off made the room warm and cosy. It brought back memories for

Winstone of those evenings as a young child when Mama and Papa sat round the lamp with him and sang songs. He wondered what they would think of a stranger in the house sitting round the lamp as they had done; a stranger who was like a brother to their son.

By the middle of December ten animals had been prepared. The water colour paint did not take well to the wood. The colours were pale but enough to distinguish the various animals. The rhinoceros was the most lifelike, with a prominent horn, followed by the elephants with their big ears. The lions were less successful, and antelope and giraffe were out of the question since their body structure was too fine to carve. There were also ten boy dolls with trousers and ten girl dolls with skirts. Absalom had excelled himself and had carved the figures with outstretched hands, so they looked more lifelike. Winstone borrowed a tarpaulin from Elias and on a Saturday morning they set out for Cheptais market.

The market was extensive with many stalls for produce, hardware, bits of machinery, bicycle parts and second-hand clothes. The noise of vendors shouting their wares and customers bargaining was overwhelming. Those with no stalls and who sold their goods from the ground had their own favourite plots. There was no room round Absalom's mum's place. They searched around for a while and had to settle for an area on the fringe of the market where it was quieter. At least it was in a location passed by many people on their way to shop.

Winstone was a little apprehensive. 'I hope people can be persuaded to stop and buy things. Adults won't want to buy any of this stuff. It will only be the kids. It will be sad if we don't sell enough to buy Ellen's uniform.'

'I know what we'll do. We'll follow Mum's example. She smiles at people as they pass and holds out her goods. We can do the same. If kids stop by, we can ask them their names. Mum says that if you get people into conversation, they are more likely to buy from you.'

Winstone had borrowed a float of small coins from Martha which he had put in a cloth bag. Just like everybody else in the market they started to engage passers-by in conversation. It was much more fun than just sitting there and hoping customers would come up to them. Some of the younger children crawled onto the tarpaulin to take a closer look at the animals and dolls. Nothing quite like their goods had been seen in the market before and because they cost relatively little, young children were able to persuade their parents to buy them a doll or an animal which they clutched proudly in their hands as they went away. Others bought paintings which they waved gaily in the air as they made for the main part of the market. The proceeds were slipped into the cloth bag which Absalom hid under the tarpaulin for safety, since theft was rife in the market. By mid-afternoon they must have chatted to three or four dozen children and parents. Many people asked why they were selling the things they had made and when they heard the proceeds were going to buy Ellen her school uniform, they were more willing to buy. Quite a number of customers praised them for their enterprise. Some of the people who came past without children even stopped and gave a donation. There came a time when there were only three animals left, one doll and one painting. Sitting in the sun for several hours and with the dust stirred up by the wind and the noise of the crowds, the boys became weary and decided to pack up.

'I think we have made quite a lot of money,' Winstone remarked.

'Better not count it out in the open,' said Absalom. 'There are always those hovering around with ill intent.'

They took themselves off to a small glade away from the market where they could be by themselves and counted out their proceeds.

'Goodness,' said Winstone, 'there's more here than I thought.'

'Me too,' agreed Absalom. 'There's quite a bit more and it isn't just from the things we made. Those donations helped.'

They had in fact raised a greater sum than the cost of a new school uniform. Winstone said they ought to celebrate by buying sodas. Sodas were a rare treat for them. Uncle John always brought sodas when he came to visit. That was the only time Absalom had tasted them. Back at the market there was a low wall outside the soda stall. They sat there swinging their legs, proud they had bought something with money they had actually earned themselves. They spent their time considering how best the rest should be spent. After Ellen's uniform had been set aside and Martha's float accounted for, Winstone calculated there was enough left to buy a second hurricane lamp which they badly needed, with the remaining few coins going to Absalom's mother to spend on food. Tired but happy they returned home after an exceptionally successful day.

Talking in bed that evening, Absalom said he couldn't believe how easily they had made so much money.

'I know some people took pity on us and gave donations, but it seems to me,' said Winstone, 'it takes only a little imagination and motivation to become rich.'

'That's probably why we are so poor,' said Absalom wistfully. 'My Dad has no imagination and the only motivation he has is to lift a glass to his mouth. The trouble is, drink numbs his brain. If he had a proper job and gave up drinking, we could live a decent life.'

'I know, it's just the same with my uncles. It's a waste of money and ruins their health but I don't think they'll ever change. It's a habit it's hard to get rid of. Grandfather says sooner or later they will suffer Divine retribution.'

'What does that mean?' asked Absalom.

'I suppose it means that they will end up in hell. Maybe when they're dead it'll be hell because they won't have a mouth to drink with and in any case, alcohol would evaporate in all that heat.'

'I think they won't go to hell. They'll go to heaven.'

'How so?'

'Well heaven is not as hot as hell, so alcohol won't evaporate as quickly and what's more there are plenty of spirits in heaven aren't there?'

Winstone laughed. 'Oh, good one, Absalom!'

CHAPTER EIGHT

The next year there was a great drought. It was hot. The sun shone ceaselessly. People waited for the rainy season to come but the rains never came. The local boys found a new means of enjoying the heat. They took up swimming. Not far from their community was a large pond made from the laterite which had been dug out of the ground to make murram roads. With its clayey bottom it always held water. Winstone's friends, Seth and Hillary had learnt to swim from one of Seth's older brothers who had attended a school in Eldoret with a swimming pool. None of the boys had swimming costumes or towels. They stripped off and jumped into the water naked and when they came out, they sat on the bank until the sun dried them. If somebody came past, they slipped into the pond again to maintain their modesty.

Absalom and Winstone joined their friends in the water. It was quite safe because the pond was shallow enough for them to stand with their heads above water and the bottom was firm. At first, they just splashed around until Seth volunteered to teach them how to swim. They picked it up quickly and were soon able to join in the races Hillary organised, swimming from one end of the pond to the other. Then when they tired of racing, they got together and held water fights. After a time, even the pond succumbed to the drought. The water evaporated in the face of the heat and became too shallow for swimming.

Elias was despondent. Cultivation of the land was at a standstill. Day after day he walked round the farm looking at the hard-baked earth, pushing his stave in and pulling it out to find that even inches under the surface it was as dry as dust. Nothing would grow in those conditions. Even the grass round the fruit trees of a variety normally resistant to drought was beginning to turn yellow. Little clouds of dust arose when the chickens scratched the ground and every day, they became more reliant on the grain given them for food. The cattle too were suffering from pasture that had dried up.

'With this lack of rain, it's impossible to sow seeds,' Elias complained to Martha. 'Our crops should normally be showing green shoots by now. Even those plants already in the soil are showing signs of distress. Their leaves are curled and turning yellow. I'm worried about the coffee crop too. I fear it could fail completely this year.'

Martha shrugged her shoulders in sympathy. 'You know, the water tank on the roof is bone dry and the water in the well is so low it's becoming impossible to fill the bucket without disturbing the mud at the bottom.'

'I know that,' replied Elias. 'I've given Winstone and Absalom instructions to drive the cows down to the river for water since we're so short of it here.'

Even the river, fed by water from the streams of Mount Elon, was in places little more than a trickle. Rocks and boulders appeared along its course which had not been seen above water in living memory. When the well on the farm dried up completely there was no alternative for the boys but to join long queues at the few remaining springs where a trickle of water was still available. Everywhere there was dust. When the wind blew there were small dust storms. Fine dust covered the leaves of plants and trees, found a resting place in people's hair, their eyes and ears and powdered washing put out to dry.

Some people blamed the lack of rain on a tribe that had moved in and denuded Mount Elgon of its trees, carrying away the wood to build houses elsewhere. Others blamed the growth of population in the area and with it the insatiable demand for firewood, leaving large stretches of land without effective tree cover. Either way it seemed the removal of trees was attributable to the lack of rain, for word had it that the one remaining forest in that part of the country had attracted violent thunder-storms and above average rainfall, causing serious flooding in the surrounding area. Then one day clouds appeared on the horizon. Peoples' expectations rose. As time went by the clouds thickened. A watery mid-day sun was obliterated by ever more menacing clouds casting an eerie light over the countryside. Expectations were replaced by feelings of unease, almost misgiving. The cows, now no longer grazing, stood motionless. The chickens ceased pecking the ground. All around the birds had stopped singing. There was no wind. The air was deathly still and apart from distant thunder heralding the approaching storm there was not a sound. All nature seemed transfixed.

Elias stood by the door looking up at the sky. 'You know Martha, I think we're in for a fearful tropical storm. I don't like the look of it at all. Those clouds are really forbidding.'

Martha came and stood by him and nodded in agreement. Caught up in the tenseness of the moment,

Winstone and Absalom left the fields and sought safety in the shelter of the farmhouse. They arrived just in time. Moments later it began to rain, not in drops but in large blobs, sparingly at first then with increasing intensity. Immediately the parched land released the sweet earthy, invigorating smell that comes after a prolonged drought. This was merely the foretaste of what was to come.

Matthew and Mark were out on the land when the rain started. 'I'm going to take cover in the house. I don't like the look of what's coming,' Matthew shouted to his brother.

'Well, I'm not,' responded Mark defiantly. 'Let it rain and thunder as much as it likes. A bit of rain and thunder didn't do anyone any harm. I'm going to see out the storm under the shelter of the trees. It's unmanly to hide away indoors.' As Matthew turned away Mark threw a stone which hit him on his back. Matthew turned around. 'Are you frightened of the storm then?' chided Mark. 'Coward!'

The lightning became more frequent and the thunder louder. Then there came a sudden rushing, chilling wind and the temperature dropped like a stone. Trees swayed wildly in the wind, their leaves flailing in the onslaught. Elias put on his jacket and the boys buttoned their shirts. Martha emerged from the bedroom with a shawl round her shoulders. All the time the storm was moving nearer, and the rain was growing more intense, beating hard on the corrugated iron roof as if it were a kettle drum.

Elias ordered the boys to close the shutters over the windows to keep out the rain and wind. It became even darker. With the shutters closed there was little light in the house. Martha lit a hurricane lamp. Lightning increased in intensity, thunder following seconds later as the storm came nearer. Suddenly there was a series of blinding flashes, brighter than the sun at mid-day. For a few seconds everything around looked as if it was alive and alight, a dancing, shimmering mirage. Simultaneously there was an indescribable explosion of thunder. Half blinded by the lightning Elias rushed from the doorway. The boys trembled in fright and Martha dashed for safety into the bedroom. For a few moments they were too stunned to say anything.

When he had regained his composure Elias said, 'That was very near. Thank the Lord it didn't strike the house. We would all have been dead. It was very close. It probably struck our land somewhere. It may have taken down a tree or two.'

By now the rain had become a cloudburst. It came down so fast it was like rods rather than drops and it hit the ground so hard it bounced up again in miniature fountains. Already the grass was under water; the hard, dry earth unable to absorb the deluge. The thunder continued to roll, reverberating in the roof. It reminded Winstone of the story of Noah, one of the many Bible stories his grandfather had instilled in him. Was this how the flood had started? When the rain began would Noah have stood in his doorway on the ark and seen the grass disappear beneath the water, then the bushes and trees, the hills and mountains until there was nothing left to see but a great sweep of water meeting the horizon? Winstone looked out of the doorway to his house across the few yards that separated it from that of his grandparent's and saw it was virtually obliterated by the rain. He hoped fervently that what he was seeing was only a storm and not the beginning of another flood.

Then the rain gave way to a hailstorm, the stones thundering down on the roof so hard you couldn't communicate even if shouting at the top of one's voice. The hail splashed on the water covering the grass with such force that the ground disappeared into a liquid haze. The boys looked on in amazement. They had never seen hail before. Then after a while the hail suddenly stopped leaving just a drizzle of rain. The boys darted outside to pick up the last few remaining balls of ice. To them it was precious. Never before had they touched ice.

Eventually, and rather reluctantly, the rain ceased. Slowly the sky lightened, the clouds rolled back, and the sun came out with sudden warmth. There was a rainbow in the sky! The air was still and as so often happens in Africa when rain comes after a long, dry spell, the atmosphere was swiftly filled with thousands of flying insects that had long lain dormant in the ground patiently awaiting life-giving moisture.

Everywhere was sodden. It would take hours if not days before the land softened and absorbed the water. From every standing object whether it be house or hut, tree or bush, water dripped. Beads of water on leaf or stem shone like diamonds in the sun. After the tumult of the storm there was a deep feeling of relief and peacefulness as if the world was taking a long deep breath, a feeling that all was forgiven. In his mind's eye Winstone imagined the storm had been God the Almighty demonstrating his unimaginable power to mere mortals on earth. They had all cowered in the face of the storm as they would before the face of God. Grandfather would have said it was a warning to those who eschewed God's laws. The peace which followed the storm and the warmth of the sun was a sign of God's benign nature and forgiveness to all who repented and followed his ways.

CHAPTER NINE

Elias stood in his doorway once again as if he was Noah surveying the land as it reappeared after the flood.

'As soon as the water has abated, I'm going around the farm to see what damage has been done,' he shouted to Martha.

Emerging from the bedroom Martha joined him by the door. 'While you do that, I shall set about getting a meal,' she replied. 'It's far too wet for any of you to work in the fields today. The boys can stay around and help me.'

Meanwhile Matthew was wondering what had happened to his brother since the storm passed. Mark had not returned home. He must be sodden, and very cold by now, Matthew thought and decided to go out to search for him. Remnants of hail stones still lay on the ground, cold to his feet. Much of the land was under a film of water. Mud oozed up between his toes as he walked. Plants in the fields were cowed from the intensity of the rain and onslaught of hail. Some had been beaten to the ground and might well die. Then as he turned, he noticed something was missing. The old sycamore fig was no more. What had been one of the grandest and most prominent trees in the landscape, one that must have been there before his father was born, had been split in two by lightning and felled almost to the ground. As he hurried over to inspect it, he saw something lying in the grass close to the charred stump.

It was Mark. He began running towards his brother shouting "Mark, Mark". When he drew close, he saw Mark's body spread-eagled in the mud. One sandal was lying a yard or so away. His shirt was split down the middle, there were burn marks on his chest and arm and his hair was singed. Matthew knelt down beside him. He was not breathing, and his body was ice cold. Feverishly he tried to resuscitate him, pressing his hands against Mark's chest and pumping hard, but to no avail. Mark too had been struck by lightning, probably the same bolt that felled the tree.

Death was staring Matthew in the face. For some moments he couldn't comprehend what had happened. The twins had been born within minutes of each other and from that moment they had never been separated. As he stared at the body, he was staring at a half of himself. It was as if he had been split in two like the sycamore fig. The thought of living without his other half was terrifying. They had always done everything together, supporting each other. They had schemed together, incited each other, relished in being bad, enjoyed irresponsibility, delighted in provoking others, savoured their notoriety and above all, believed they were indomitable and irreproachable. Suddenly Matthew felt terribly alone. Their power and their security in the way they behaved lay in living and acting as a pair, the power of two over the power of one. Now, as an individual with an unsavoury reputation and no twin to support him, everyone would be his enemy. His security was no more. Plagued by these thoughts and the horror of loss and death, he ran screaming to his parents.

In the house everyone froze at the sound of Matthew's screaming, screaming like a madman. Matthew, his body spattered with mud from head to foot burst through the doorway where he broke into a flood of tears shouting, 'He's dead! Mark's dead! Struck by lightning! What am I to do? What am I to do?'

For a moment nobody spoke, shocked into silence. Then Elias put his arms round Matthew who seemed as if at any moment he would collapse on the floor and without saying a word dragged him over to a chair and sat him down. Matthew, his face in his hands, was so choked with crying he couldn't speak. Martha came running back from the kitchen in tears, put her arms around Matthew and stroked his forehead to try to calm him. Absalom was not only shocked but felt decidedly awkward and out of place. He had never seen an adult cry in that manner before. He had seen his mother weep tears many times when she was without money, yet those were gentle tears, tears of resignation which encouraged him to put his arms round her shoulders to comfort her. But this was wild crying, tears of anger, of fear and hopelessness. Absalom was embarrassed. This was not his family, nor his household nor even his relatives. He had no right to be there. This was a family matter in which he ought to have no part. He was wondering whether he should leave when he turned and saw Winstone cowering in a corner, trying to hide his tears. For Winstone, Matthew's grieving brought back still raw memories of his mother's grieving over the death of his father and his own grieving at the loss of his mother. Absalom had never seen Winstone weep. He went straight way to comfort him and then realised he was not without a role in this family tragedy.

When eventually Matthew calmed down, he and Elias walked back to where Mark's body lay. Winstone and Absalom were forbidden to follow them. Instead, they accompanied Martha back to the kitchen since she was in no state to prepare a meal on her own. Matthew and Elias made an improvised stretcher out of a tarpaulin and two poles and carried Mark's body back to his house. Then later that day, still in a state of shock, Elias cycled into Cheptais to summon the rest of the family to Mark's funeral. It would be a few days before all could be assembled so Elias arranged with the clinic for somebody to come to preserve the body with formalin until the funeral was held.

Not only was Elias despondent at the loss of another son, no matter how bad Mark might have been, Elias was desolate at the thought of having to run the farm almost entirely by himself. It was a daunting if not impossible task in his advancing years.

'I fear for the future,' he confided in Martha. 'I've worked so hard to make this place a success, saved to buy additional land to make it a profitable enterprise and hand it on to my sons as my father handed it to me and now, I'm left with just myself and one useless son. With every year I grow older I shall be able to do less until there comes a time when most of the land will be uncultivated. Then how shall we live? What income shall I have? John won't come back to farm it. He's an experienced town dweller. His job pays well, and he won't want to give it up. Crispin has a good job too and there would be little incentive for him to come back here and be confined to rural isolation when he has been used to travelling the length and breadth of the country. Even the next generation won't be interested. Winstone is bright. He won't stay here. John's children have never lived in the countryside and will never wish to.'

Martha had no liking for church and rarely attended services, but she nonetheless had a strong faith. 'You are worrying yourself unnecessarily,' she maintained. 'Where is your faith? Isn't that why you go to church? Pessimism never got anybody anywhere. You never know what the future holds. Things could just as well turn out alright in the end.'

During the time between Mark's death and his funeral Matthew stayed in his own home in solitary confinement and refused to come outside. Martha brought him some broth which he accepted but despite her persistence he refused to eat a proper meal. The funeral itself was a relatively quiet affair. Elias was well supported by the church's congregation but apart from the family, few attended the burial on Mark's plot of land. Absalom's mother was there, as were the families of Seth and Hillary, Andrew and Kelvin, Winstone's closest friends, largely to support Winstone himself in the face of another death in the family. Elias felt slighted because the majority of his neighbours did not attend the burial whereas in reality it was not a show of disrespect for him but a recognition of their disapproval of the twins.

After the funeral Matthew again retired to his house and apart from Martha when she brought him broth, refused to see anyone else. The storm had been followed by a succession of sun and showers and although it was already late in the season the planting had to be done. With the funeral over, Crispin delayed returning to his job in order to help Elias and the boys to do as much planting as they could, Elias and Crispin working during the day and Winstone and Absalom assisting before school and after they returned home later in the day. By now the soil had recovered from being flooded.

It turned easily under the plough, rich brown fertile soil ready to bear the seed for the forthcoming crops. Meanwhile Martha prepared evening meals for all of them so that neither the boys nor Crispin had to return to their homes to prepare their own food. With the drought and its intense heat gone it was pleasant to sit outside of an evening in the moist warm air under a starlit sky and while away the time in idle conversation.

One evening when Elias and Crispin were sitting on their own, Crispin turned to his father and said, 'Dad, I've decided to give up my job.'

Elias was surprised. This was a turn of events he hadn't anticipated.

'Decided to give up your job? Why ever would you want to do that?'

'It's not that I don't like the job,' said Crispin, 'I relish seeing all the different parts of our country. It's just so varied. You've got the tropical coastline where it's always hot and sticky and - oh, did you know the sea is full of salt?'

'Full of salt? No, I didn't know that. What a waste of water!' his father observed. 'You can't use saltwater for irrigation, and you can't drink it. It's good for nothing.'

'The fish enjoy it,' quipped Crispin. 'Then if you go to the top of Mount Kenya there's snow lying there all the year round. Yet down in the rift valley there are lakes of hot water which attract birds called flamingos. They're pink in colour and there are hundreds of them. Seen from a distance it looks as if the water has turned pink. Some of the pools are so hot you can put eggs in a bag and boil them. And then up in the north there are large areas of desert where it is too hot and dry to grow anything. Some of the desert is sand with no landmarks at all and unless you follow the tracks of other vehicles you would never know where the road was. In other parts it is just small round boulders, hundreds and thousands of them strewn over the ground looking like fields of cabbages from a distance and you have to keep to a track that has been cleared by others otherwise you would never pass through them,' Crispin recounted with enthusiasm. 'You really ought to see them, Dad.'

'No thank you,' his father said, disparagingly. 'I'm quite content to remain here where the land is green and fertile and gives me a reasonable living. Travelling isn't for me. I don't even like being in John's car. You can keep your deserts and your snow and saltwater. What good is any of it to me? Anyway, why do you want to give up your job? It pays well doesn't it?'

'Yes, it pays well but you know, I'm thirty now. All my friends are married and

I shan't find a wife while I spend all my time in the cab of a lorry. Oh yes, I know, I often pass girls thumbing a lift, but they aren't looking for a ride on a lorry, they're looking for a man to ride on them! So, I've decided to hand in my notice and come to work on the farm. I can see now how much you need my help and maybe I'll find a local girl to be my wife.'

After Mark's funeral his house was abandoned as is the tradition when a man is single. Then one evening there was a knock at Winstone's door. The boys were doing their homework at the time. Winstone was surprised. It wasn't a knock he recognised. Everybody knocked in a different manner. Grandfather's knock was hard and urgent. Grandmother's knock was more gentle, but nevertheless determined. But this knock was kind of timid, as if it wasn't sure of itself.

Winstone went to the door and opened it. At first, in the darkness, he couldn't be sure who was there. Then he recognised the person and his heart raced. It was Matthew, but not the Matthew he knew. His head was bowed. He looked thin and bedraggled. He didn't look up when the door was opened. He remained staring at his feet.

There was a long pause and then Winstone said, 'Come in.'

Matthew shuffled in and Winstone shut the door behind him. Absalom caught Winstone's eye. They were both wondering what to say.

Then without looking up Matthew spoke. 'I've come to ask forgiveness,' he confessed. 'Forgiveness for how I've treated you. I've come to realise how wicked Mark and I have been to you and to everyone else. I don't want to have enemies around me. I don't want people to hate me. I don't want to be an outcast. I don't want people to turn away from me. I want to reform. I want to be a good person. I want to be loved.'

There was a pause. Matthew continued to stare at the floor. Winstone did not know how to respond. This was a proud, male-orientated society where men were considered to be superior to women and children. Yet here was a man, an uncle at that, and one Winstone had feared, standing before an eleven-year-old asking a child for his forgiveness. Those last few words, "I want to be loved" drove deep into Winstone's heart. He remembered the times after his parents had died how he had longed to be loved and the desolation he had felt when love was not forthcoming. Now he had love, not love in the form of kissing and hugging but a companionship he shared with Absalom so deep that it substituted for love. Next moment, without really thinking, he had flung his arms round Matthew's waist and buried his head in Matthews chest. Slowly Matthew raised his arms and wrapped them round Winstone's back.

'Shall I go and make some tea?' Absalom asked, his words bringing normality back to an awkward situation.

Winstone released his arms and straightened up, said it was a good idea and told him to take the second hurricane lamp with him. Winstone did not know what to say. He drew up a chair and persuaded Matthew to sit down. They sat in silence for a while, Matthew staring at the floor. Winstone shuffled uneasily in his chair and then Matthew started to talk again.

'You know,' he said, 'your mother was a lovely woman. When your father married her, we were jealous. We didn't think he deserved such a fine woman. Then when your father died, and your mother left we felt bitter. We felt she had snubbed us, that she thought she was too good for us and we took our revenge out on you. It was a stupid thing to do. It must have made you very unhappy. You have had enough sadness in your life without us making it worse. We have been unkind to our father too. We have never really helped him when he needed it and we have been rude and abusive to him which sons should never have been. Now I want to make amends. I want to give up drinking. I want to become a good son and a good farmer. I'm desperate for people to respect me.'

Absalom arrived with mugs of tea. Winstone was relieved. He did not know how to reply to Matthew. Absalom's intervention saved his embarrassment.

'How many sugars?' asked Absalom cheerily.

Winstone was never more glad than now, to have Absalom sharing his home. He could not have managed this encounter on his own. Absalom possessed a natural exuberance in contrast to Winstone's cautious, pensive attitude to life. In a way their separate personalities complemented each other, the one cheerful and reassuring, the other the tactician and organiser. Matthew added two spoonfuls to his tea. Absalom pushed a mug towards Winstone and took the third for himself. Then he pulled a packet of biscuits out of his anorak pocket. Biscuits were a rare treat.

Winstone turned to Absalom. 'Wherever did you get those from?'

'Ah ha! Well, I thought Matthew looked hungry so while the water was boiling, I thought I would slip over to your grandmother to ask whether she had anything for him to eat. She pulled this packet out of a drawer. She said it was one Uncle John had brought her and she had saved it for a special occasion, and this is a special occasion isn't it? It says on the packet "Chocolate Digestive Biscuits". Should be good!'

Matthew was reluctant to go to his parent's house. He felt drained after making his confession to Winstone and went back home taking most of the biscuits with him. Instead, the boys went over to Elias and Martha and told them what Matthew had said to them. Martha said she was not surprised her son didn't come over with them.

'Let him have time to overcome the shock of losing his brother,' she said. 'He'll come to see us when he's ready. It's early days yet.'

Elias said the shock must have made him change his attitude to life and it would be a miracle if he really meant what he said about becoming a good farmer. It prompted Martha with her sharp tongue to scold Elias in front of the boys.

'There, what did I tell you,' she said. 'Didn't I say you were a pessimist Elias! Didn't I say you lacked faith?

Didn't I say things would turn out alright? Didn't I say you would have help on the farm?'

CHAPTER TEN

Tortured by the death of his parents and then by the behaviour of his twin uncles Winstone's early years from the age of four had been coloured by sorrow, loneliness and fear. Then as a school pupil and with his close friendship with Absalom, his life had begun to change for the better. After Mark died it seemed as if the dark clouds of his early years were a thing of the past and with Matthew's change of character, Winstone believed the sun had once again begun to shine in his life. By the time he was twelve he was no longer seen as a burden by his grandparents, for there were two other adults capable of looking after him. With Crispin, Matthew and the boys working in close harmony on the land Elias, relieved of much of his workload, was able to turn his attention to the overall running of the farm. As an unmarried man, Crispin had saved enough of his earnings to buy a second-hand van which he used to take produce to Cheptais. He also persuaded Absalom's mother to give up dealing in clothes and instead sell their produce from a stall he set up in the market.

Since Crispin had no children of his own, he took a particular interest in the two boys. Meals were often taken in his house, and even if Winstone and Absalom prepared their own food they often went over to spend the evenings with Crispin and Matthew. It was obviously something they both appreciated since neither of them had grown up in a close family relationship.

Before Absalom came to live with him Winstone had lived a lonely life and Absalom himself had never had a close relationship with his older brothers and sisters, nor indeed with his father. Now everybody had come together as a real farming family with Elias and Crispin taking the helm and Matthew, Winstone and Absalom the able crew.

Being part of a family again since his early childhood helped to overcome Winstone's anguish at losing his parents. He now felt happier than he had ever been since their loss. He had security and friendship. He was well fed and well looked after. He enjoyed working as part of a team on the farm and he loved his schoolwork and the time he spent painting and drawing in a home of his own. Absalom too, was glad to be an accepted member of the family for by now he was no longer treated as an outsider but looked upon almost as another brother. Both boys had gained much from their friendship. By sharing their lives and supporting each other they were developing into confident and mature young people. Nevertheless, even in this homely atmosphere Winstone could never entirely forget the loss of his mother and father and every now and again an incident cropped up which reignited the sorrows of the past.

It was the summer holidays. Each boy had been given a piece of land all to themselves on which they could cultivate whatever took their fancy. Crispin had said it was an opportunity for them to demonstrate how well they could manage their plot without supervision and how imaginative they could be in the plants they chose to grow. It was a challenge they had accepted readily. In fact, it became something of a competition. For once they agreed not to share everything, each deciding in secret what they were going to cultivate, buying seeds with money given them by Crispin. Besides planting a few staple crops, Winstone decided to do something exceptional and grow flowers for cutting. It wasn't the custom for people to use flowers for decorating their homes but he thought it was a nice idea even though the cultivation of flowers was considered a waste of good agricultural land. He couldn't buy seeds locally so in secret he had asked John to bring him some seeds the next time he was in Nairobi. Absalom also had the idea of grow something unusual. He too had turned to John to get him some herb seeds which were rarely grown and would take up relatively little space. John was amused that both boys had confided in him without them realising it. As was their custom, John and his family had come to stay for a week or so on the farm in the school holidays. By now Winstone was bordering thirteen, Petra almost fifteen, Michael a bit younger and Jamie, the baby, nearly nine. It was a warm sunny day. The whole family had just finished a meal outside. Absalom had taken Michael and Jamie down to the river to splash around in the water. Winstone and Petra remained with the adults.

'Why don't you take Petra to see your new piece of land and show her what you've planted?' suggested Crispin. 'Everything will soon be ready for harvesting.'

The two of them got up and set off for the far end of the farm where Winstone's land lay. Petra was impressed when she saw what Winstone had achieved, yet conscious of her seniority, being two years older than Winstone, and she believed, more worldly-wise than a mere country boy, she always felt the need to exercise what she considered was her superior knowledge and use it to put him in his place.

'If I had been you,' she said, 'I would've planted fewer sweet potatoes and more Irish potatoes and I would've planted more tomatoes and beans and less kale. I hate the stuff anyway. But I like the way you've planted those flowers for cutting. I think it's nice to have some flowers in the house.'

Winstone thought that was small praise indeed. Petra, forthright and out outspoken in her manner was not the least bit prudish. After walking around the plot, she announced she needed a wee and immediately squatted down on the side of the field. Winstone was shocked by her lack of modesty. He had not seen anybody act like that before. In the countryside apart from young children, going to the toilet was a very private affair. There were occasions when he might pee outside, but one always made sure of being out of the sight of others. Besides, you always peed standing up, and not like she was doing. When she got back on her feet Winstone asked why she urinated squatting down. Petra looked at him and said with incredulity. 'Cos we don't have a penis!'

'Don't women have penises?'

'Of course not, silly.'

This news came as a revelation to Winstone. He found it difficult to believe. He was rebuffed by Petra's know-all tone of voice. How could it be that he had lived twelve years without knowing this basic piece of information?

'Why don't women have penises?'

'Because women have babies, don't you know?'

'Of course, I know. But if you can manage without a penis why do men have them?'

'To put their seed into a woman so she gets a baby.'

'You mean to say a man has to put seed into a woman for her to get a baby?'

'Of course. He puts his seed into a woman in a hole between her legs - the same hole the baby comes out of. Didn't you know that?'

Winstone looked very uncomfortable. 'But,' he stammered, 'I thought a woman had a baby because she was loved by a man. I thought loving and kissing is what made a baby grow in a woman.'

'My goodness, you're an innocent aren't you! Everything starts from seed. Surely you know that! Don't you plant seeds in the ground to make plants grow? And don't you pull them out of the ground when they are fully grown, just like a baby is pulled out of a woman? Don't trees have seeds? Haven't you seen animals mating? Where have you been all your life?'

'Yes, but plants don't love each other, trees don't love each other, and animals don't love each other. You mean to say we... we're no better than animals?'

'Yes.'

'But I thought humans were above animals. I thought we were above mating. I thought, as superior beings, it was love that made us humans.'

'We're above animals because of our intelligence. We're the most intelligent beings on earth. More intelligent than dogs, or elephants or cheetahs. We're sort-of civilised in a way they can't be. That's why we can control everything.'

'So, you mean my father and mother had to have sex for me to be born, just as if they were animals?'

'Yes.'

'I didn't realise.' For a moment Winstone was lost for words. 'But my mother couldn't have sex with another man after she had had sex with my father because they loved each other very much?'

'Oh yes she could!'

'Even if they didn't love each other?'

'Yes, of course. Animals don't have to love each other to mate and nor do humans.'

'So, love isn't important then?'

'Depends upon how you feel about it.'

'But a bull can mate a cow even if the cow doesn't want to be mated.'

'So, can a man mate with a woman even if she doesn't want it. That's what's called rape.'

'But that's terrible! So, a child could be born without being loved by its father and the father could just go away and never see his child. Then... we're just like animals!'

'Yes!'

'But I always believed humans loved each other and that God loved us.'

'So, what about your twin uncles then. Did they love you?'

'No, that's true. But there's always to be some wicked people around because if there were no wicked people how would we know who good people were? That's why we have evil in the world because if we didn't have evil, we couldn't experience goodness. We wouldn't know what goodness was.'

'I would've thought your grandfather would've told you the story about Adam and Eve.'

'He did.'

'Well, you couldn't have listened properly. When Adam ate that apple, we all became a bit wicked.'

'But I've always tried to be a good person and I know my mother was a good person and so was my father. Many people loved them.'

What Petra had told him stunned Winstone. A whole new dimension to his mother's going away had opened up before him. A day that had started out so happily had now turned his thoughts into the deepest sorrow. Inwardly he was crying for his mother. What if she wasn't dead? After his father died what if she had gone off with another man without taking him with her? What if she had children by him, born of his own dear mother? There could be half brothers and sisters in the world that he did not know about and might never meet; children who would regard him as a stranger if they did meet, or perhaps would never know he existed. What if she loved them, doted on them, hugged and kissed them more than she had loved him? Had she loved him so much before she disappeared simply because she felt guilty at leaving him? Or worse still, had she been made to have sex against her will by some man who had molested her. Grandfather had often said that women should be protected, that it was dangerous for them to go out on their own into crowds they didn't know, that women needed a husband to protect them. If she had gone away by herself without another man, she would have been so vulnerable. She might have had children against her will. She might have had children she didn't love and if there was no husband to provide for her, she could be living in poverty.

Absalom had enjoyed being accepted by the whole of his adopted family. Michael and Jamie had delighted in his company and after cooling off on the banks of the river they had gone on an expedition to some high rocks not far away where each of them had hidden in turn and then had to be found by the others. Michael was at an age when he was beginning to feel the need of a degree independence. Being in the company of Absalom, who let him roam as he wished, he enjoyed a freedom and the liberty he would not have had in his parent's company.

Jamie was fond of Absalom. He insisted on holding Absalom's hand when they walked along and implored him to let him sit on his shoulders, which he did from time to time, holding firmly onto Jamie's legs so that he didn't fall off when they crossed over rough ground. Jamie loved it when Absalom picked him up and flung him over his shoulder, legs in the air and head upside-down behind his bearer's back. Absalom enjoyed being with these two fun-loving youngsters too, and wished he had younger brothers of his own. Since that was not to be, he would have to wait until he had his own children, but not too many, two or three at the most. He thought of his father with anguish. Why had he decided to bring nine children into the world when he couldn't provide adequately for those he already had? Why did he decide to have so many? He knew these days there were ways of stopping women from having kids. Was he being selfish by believing that when he grew old and infirm, he would ensure there would be enough of his children to look after him? That was in any case an outdated concept. Far fewer children died at birth and in childhood now that clinics and hospitals were available to treat them. What his father had done was to compromise the quality of life of his offspring. With so many mouths to feed and kids to clothe, life had been a continuous struggle for survival for all of them. That he knew from his own experience. There was no money to pay for medication when they fell ill. Of the younger ones, all had to make do with hand-me-down shorts, trousers and dresses. None had shoes to wear. Most of them had gone to school hungry at one time or another, and he remembered the disappointment on the faces of his siblings when their friends had gone off on school trips and they had to remain behind because there was no money to pay for them. It wasn't as if his father cared for his wife and her wellbeing, nor for his children for that matter. He had virtually abandoned them while they were growing up, inciting bitterness in their minds at his lack of interest in them. Absalom understood the anguish Winstone endured through losing his parents, but his own experience had been little better with a father who ignored him, and a mother made miserable at the hands of her husband.

When Absalom returned home in the evening, he found Winstone alone in the house. He was eager to regale him with their adventures, but he found Winstone uncommunicative.

'What's the matter? Got a headache or something?'

Winstone shook his head. 'No, I'm alright.'

'You bet you are. What's getting you?'

'Oh, it's nothing. It's just something Petra said.'

'Come on, what did she say? Surely she didn't say something you can't tell me?'

Winstone bit his lip. He felt such an idiot not knowing something that everybody else knew about. What would Absalom think of him if he confessed his innocence?

'It was something personal,' he said, trying to stave off further questions.

'I thought we had agreed to share everything with each other, so what are you holding back for?'

Winstone was well aware they had made that agreement and he realised that if he did not honour it, he would break the trust they had in each other. 'It's that sex thing,' he volunteered.

'She didn't try to make love to you, did she?'

That brought a smile to Winstone's face.

'No, she didn't. I couldn't imagine being in love with her. She's too much of a know-all, and because I'm younger than her she's always trying to put me down. Absalom, you'll think I'm dumb, but I never knew about sex. I never knew girls didn't have a penis. I never knew a man had to put seed into a woman for her to have a baby. I thought just loving each other was enough for a woman to have a child. Did you know about this?'

Absalom chuckled. 'Yes, of course I knew. I've got a sister, haven't I? You get to know all about these things when you've got a girl in the house. Trouble is, you've never lived in a family. What I didn't see for myself my older brothers told me. I was really quite shocked at the time and that was bad enough hearing it from brothers. It must have been worse hearing it from a girl.'

'I suppose that explains then while I get funny feelings in my private parts from time to time, I never related it to the difference between men and women. I just thought it was a nice thing to happen.'

'You're right. That little friend has a mind of its own. Sometimes it's quite out of control. One day, my brothers told me, it'll start to produce seed.'

'I wonder what it will be like?'

Absalom laughed. 'Wet, I should think. My brothers said there aren't any words to describe the feeling. They said it was just absolutely fantastic.'

'I'm worried about my mother though,' said Winstone. 'Petra said it was possible for any man to give her a baby whether she was married to him and loved him or not or whether she was forced into having a baby by a man who didn't stay with her. I believed she loved me more than anyone else after my father died. Is that why she left me so suddenly? Could there be another man she had fallen in love with? Supposing she did have another man and had children which she loved. I would feel terribly left out. I would feel totally abandoned. In fact, I would rather die than have that happen. There could be any number of half brothers and sisters that I don't know about. It's a horrible thought - the thought of being abandoned by a mother I love and who I thought loved me. Just thinking about it makes me feel very upset. I can't get the idea out of my mind. It's churning round and round in my head, stirring up grief, desolation, desertion.' Tears started to well up in his eyes. 'It's not just that I feel a fool not knowing about sex, it's that I can't be sure whether she's alive or not and if she is alive, where she is and who she's with and whether there are other children she loves and if so where are they?'

Tears were rolling down his cheeks. He tried to wipe them away on the sleeve of his shirt. His distress related not only to the things he had learnt that afternoon, and the uncertainty over his mother's motives, but also as the organiser and instigator in their partnership he had secretly thought himself superior to Absalom. Now he had to come to terms with the fact that this was a delusion. He was not superior in any way, and instead had to rely on Absalom's compassion for a shoulder to cry on.

Absalom understood how Winstone felt. He would have been just as distraught himself had he been in the same circumstances. But being the cheerful optimist and mature beyond his years Absalom could see there was an alternative scenario to the one his friend envisaged. He put his arm round Winstone's shoulder.

'Look here,' he said. 'You said your mother loved you dearly. No mother would abandon a child she really loved for another person. Your grandmother said she was dead; I think she was right. I think she went away because she knew she was going to die. That was a very generous and kind thing to do. It showed her very great love for you. How would it have felt if you had found your mother dead? How would you have felt if you had to attend another funeral with all those mourners, all that speech making, all that wailing? And there would have been many there because she was much loved. You would have been all by yourself. How would you have felt seeing her body lowered into the ground and covered with earth? She went away to save you all that anguish. That was the kindest and most loving thing a mother could do. Don't you understand?'

Winstone brightened. A smile crept across his face. How could it be that Absalom had this knack of being so positive in the face of life's vicissitudes despite all the difficulties he had experienced in his family home, while he himself seemed always to be drawn to morbid introspection? Was it his prolonged loneliness that led him to be morose or was it the uncertainty surrounding his mother's disappearance, the lack of closure to the most momentous event in his life? He was certain of his father's death, but what of his mother? It was Absalom's ebullience which made Winstone feel ashamed of himself and it was with relief he flung his arms around Absalom.

'You're right,' he said. 'I was depressed and concentrated on all the bad things that could happen and not the good things. You've helped to make me convinced of my mother's love for me. Imagine what it would be like for me if I didn't have you for company. It would have weighed on my mind forever. I don't think I would ever have got through with it plaguing my mind.'

'Tell you what,' Absalom said, drawing away and changing the subject. 'Let's make a pact that we tell each other when we each produce that seed for the first time and get that wonderful feeling.'

Changing the subject was Absalom's typical way of clearing the air, as it were, and refreshing one's thoughts.

'That's a great idea. There mustn't ever be any secrets between us. It's a mark of our friendship and we must make it a pact! Let's shake on it.'

CHAPTER ELEVEN

Elias was attending a meeting of the parent-teacher association at the primary school. He was a much-respected member of the group since all six of his children had attended the school. Now he had returned as guardian of both Absalom and Winstone. After the meeting finished the headmaster Mr Murunga invited Elias into his office. Elias and Martin Murunga were good friends and Martin said that since both boys were now in Standard Eight and would be leaving school at the end of the year he wanted to talk to Elias about their future.

'I shall be sorry to lose those two pupils,' he said. 'They're both outstanding in their different ways. Absalom has become a good all-round sportsman. I find it astonishing that a boy who was such a weakling when he first came to us should now be one of our top performers. That's all due to you Elias for taking him in and looking after him so well.'

'Well,' Elias explained, 'It wasn't me who instigated it. It was Winstone who begged me to let Absalom come to live with us after that incident on the playing field. I was opposed to the idea at first, I have to confess, but it was the right decision in the end.'

'Absalom's a great kid, clever but not as academically bright as Winstone. He will do well at our secondary school if you or his mother can find the fees for him. However, Winstone is outstanding, clever in every subject. In all my years of teaching I've had only two pupils to equal him, one of whom won a place at a top school in Nairobi. If I were to be honest with you, he's "national" school material. If he sat an exam for one of those schools, I'm sure he would be accepted. Looking at it selfishly, I have to say, it would be a tremendous boost for our school if he got in and no doubt raise the morale of my pupils. Having said that, Elias, I am very well aware that the fees at national schools are high and for that reason exclude most candidates from the rural areas. That's why I wanted to have a chat with you. We're old friends. I'm sure you never expected to educate a grandson, especially one as exceptional as Winstone and I fear I may have put you in a predicament. D'you think there is any way you could raise the fees?'

Elias thought about it for a moment. 'I knew Winstone was clever, but I never realised he was that clever. It's come as a bit of a shock. That would mean fees for the four years of his secondary education. Then what? University I suppose, but I would never be able to afford that.'

'Since Winstone is an orphan, the government may step in to support him at university.'

'Yes, I suppose so,' said Elias, 'but the problem with that is we can't prove he's an orphan because we can't be sure that his mother is dead. We have no record.'

'That could be a problem but there may be ways of getting around it.'

'Well, as you know, John has a good job in Eldoret, and Crispin will have some savings from his time as a lorry driver and now that Catherine is nursing in Kisumu, she may be able to make a contribution. As for me, things are better than they were now that Crispin and Matthew work full time on the farm, but there's a lot of competition in the market for fruit and vegetables. We score over the others because we have our own stall and Absalom's mother is a pleasant woman and attracts customers. She's also a dab hand at setting out her goods and making them look attractive - and our produce is very fresh since Crispin drives in every day with a new supply. Nevertheless, we don't make as much profit as I would like.'

'Would you think of holding a *harambee* to raise funds?' Martin volunteered. 'We could involve the school and maybe you could involve the church as well as local people. I could invite our MP. I doubt whether he would come. These politicians are busy people, but he might be prepared to give a donation.' 'That's a thought,' said Elias. 'I wish Delia was still with us. She would've been clever at arranging a *harambee* and she was so much liked locally that people would have had no hesitation in attending. Of course, we couldn't hold an event like that until we knew Winstone had a place at a school.'

'Very true. But if he does get a place, I know several parents in the school who have experience in arranging *harambees*. I'm sure I could persuade them to help if the need arises.'

'Obviously I shall have to discuss this with Martha and John and the others and, Martin, would you advise me having a word with Winstone himself about all this?'

'Yes, you should. I think he would jump at the idea if he's not unhappy at the prospect of leaving home.'

When Elias spoke to John about his conversation with Martin, John said the time he saw Delia after Jeremiah's burial she said Winstone would be a clever child and wanted him to do well and be a credit to his father. That information led Elias to believe a place at a national school was probably the right outcome for Winstone.

One evening a few days later Elias called Winstone and Absalom over to his house. He and Martha sat down with the boys.

'We've been thinking about your future,' Elias began. 'The other day I had a chat with your headmaster, Mr. Murunga. Now that you're on the point of leaving primary school, he thinks you should both continue your education. He admires you Absalom as a sportsman. He also believes you're good educational material and should go on to the secondary school in Cheptais. I'm aware Absalom, that I don't pay you anything for the work you do for me on the farm. You've helped a lot. I'm appreciative of what you've done. You've really put your back into your work, and I'm grateful to you. So, to make up for it, I've resolved to pay for your secondary education for the four years you'll be at school.'

Absalom had not anticipated continuing with his education. After all, neither his mother nor his father were in a position to pay for his secondary schooling. They had no land to speak of, so even subsistence farming was out of the question. The best he had thought he could do for himself was to get a job in a local store in Cheptais or perhaps join the police force. For a few moments he just stared at Elias, hardly believing what he had heard. Then, 'Wow,' he exclaimed. 'I never thought I would have a chance to go to secondary school given my mother's financial situation. I thought it would be out of reach. That's fantastic news! I'm ever so grateful to you.'

Martha chipped in with her familiar matter-of-fact tone of voice, 'It's well deserved. You've helped my husband at a time when he really needed it. You've worked hard and have contributed a lot to our farm. We're pleased with you.'

Winstone glanced at Absalom, full of admiration. He was grateful too, for the regard his parents had for his friend, a vindication of Absalom coming to live with him.

'As for you, Winstone, Mr Muranga advises you sit for an entry exam for a national school. You would sit for the exam at school here, but of course there's no guarantee you would pass. If you did pass it would mean leaving home and going to a boarding school. How would you feel about that?'

Winstone had assumed he would go to school in Cheptais. The thought of going away to a boarding school had never occurred to him.

'Going to a boarding school wouldn't bother me,' he said. 'What would bother me is leaving Absalom here on his own.'

'Don't let that worry you,' Absalom said generously. 'Your company in the holidays would more than compensate for your absence in term time, and in any case, I won't be lonely since I shall still have all my school friends.'

The decision was made. It was agreed Winstone would sit an exam for a national school and Absalom would begin at the local secondary school the following January.

It was August, and as it was an even-dated year, it was a year when among Winstone's people, boys were circumcised. Boys were free to choose when they went through the ceremony but peer pressure usually led to their early teens. Seth, and his half-brother Hillary, opted to be circumcised that August. They invited Winstone and Absalom to join the cheer leaders' group which would support them throughout the ritual over a period of several days. Winstone asked whether he and Absalom could be circumcised at the same time, but Elias ruled it out.

'As much as I think you should go through the ritual now, I really can't afford it. Traditional circumcisions are very expensive events. It is not just the cost of providing food and drink for family and friends, it's all the many uninvited guests who will turn up. They too will expect to be provided for, since it's a time of great celebration you know. It could cost a fortune. You see, just in case you get a place at a national school I'll need every shilling I have, and more besides, to put towards your fees. But let's hope we could arrange something another year.'

In a way Winstone was glad his circumcision was postponed. The ritual was very much a family affair and as an orphan, circumcision without his parent's presence was always going to magnify his anguish at their absence.

Absalom and Winstone were part of a group of about eight boys, most of them already circumcised, who accompanied Seth and Hillary as they danced at various neighbouring homes inviting the householders to attend the event. They also followed them on the day before circumcision when covered in flour paste, and naked but for a pair of shorts, and in bare feet, the boys separated to dance at their respective maternal families, Seth and Hillary's father having married two wives. Winstone and Absalom had seen many circumcision ceremonies before, so they were not at a loss as to what they should do. The cheer group split in two and followed them, chanting songs of encouragement, blowing whistles and clearing the paths of approaching people. It was a long and exhausting day especially since each boy had to stop and be chastised by being slapped on the face and spat on many times by the relatives they visited, in order to determine how manly they were. It was a disgrace if they fell to crying or indeed showing any kind of fear.

A bull was slaughtered at their maternal homes and each boy was allowed to eat and rest for a time. Their manliness was tested again by throwing in their face the undigested food of the slaughtered bull. The smell was objectionable, and the stomach acid stung their eyes. Then came the final run back to their home to dance with the neighbours until the small hours. Exhausted, they were allowed a short rest until pre-dawn when they were once more on the move, this time naked, down to the river to be smeared from head to foot with mud, still cold from the night air, their only anaesthetic before circumcision took place. Running naked in the midst of so many followers was an ordeal for boys coming from a prudish society where sex was rarely talked about in the family and children were banned even from entering their parent's bedrooms. Winstone thought that when his time came to go through the ritual it was that aspect that would have worried him more than the final procedure.

At the final run home, a great crowed awaited them. Seth and Hillary's maternal and paternal grandparents, aunts and uncles and all their offspring were there in full force as were several dozen neighbours. The boys ran back just as the sun rose above the horizon and with arms held high to signal they were not afraid of the ensuing pain, the circumcisers moved in swiftly to perform the operation. Blood was spilled, and a roar of approval arose from the assembled company.

Being in the cheer group, Winstone was able to observe every aspect of the ritual. By now he had honed his ability to make quick sketches and armed with pencils and drawing pad he recorded many of the events as they occurred: male guests sitting round a communal bowl of beer drinking through long straws, the slaughtering of a bull, Seth and Hillary running down to the river and being covered with mud, the cheer group as it followed the boys home and finally the circumcision.

At the time Winstone did not realise the importance of what he was doing. Nobody in those rural areas possessed a camera. His sketches which he later worked up into watercolour paintings became some of the first permanent records of these ceremonies and were much in demand in later life. Some days later Winstone showed his sketches to Seth and Hillary. They were impressed by them and wanted to have copies.

'Was the circumcision painful?' he asked.

'Not to begin with,' Hillary said. 'The knives were very sharp and when you're first cut you don't feel it. The pain comes a little while after and then it's really painful.'

'It's a good thing the pain is delayed because we no longer have to look brave in front of all those people,' added Seth.

'But what's worse is when they put a powder on the wound as a disinfectant,' recounted Hillary with feeling. 'Wow, we just curled up with pain then.'

By the end of the holidays Seth and Hillary's wounds had healed and they were enjoying the respect their elders accorded them now they were considered as men.

In his last term at primary school Winstone sat his entry exam. It was October before the result came through. When it was announced in school, he had won a place at a national school in Nairobi, his fellow classmates cheered.

Back home Elias, Martha, John, Crispin, Catherine and Matthew began to plan the *harambee*. It was to be held over a weekend when they were all free. Mr Murunga agreed to notify the parents of children at school and would send a personal invitation to the member of parliament. Elias had asked the pastor to give out a notice in church and Absalom and Winstone were detailed to visit all the families in the community who were not connected with either church or school with a personal invitation to the event. So that there was some indication of numbers, both the church and the school asked people to let them know if they were going to attend.

Elias was thankful his people were eaters of chicken rather than meat. He reckoned there were enough chickens on the farm to feed everybody. The harvest had been excellent that year, so he had a goodly supply of maize-meal and vegetables. Normally the cost of providing food and drink for the attendees would have been considerable but on this occasion the only major outlay was going to be the provision of beer.

On the day of the *harambee* Winstone and Absalom restocked the kitchen with firewood in preparation for all the cooking which had to be done and gathered together as many chairs as they could for people to sit on, even borrowing from neighbours. They also laid out tarpaulins on the ground for children to sit on, while Crispin and Matthew dug up and prepared the maize and vegetables. Meanwhile Martha and Miriam were detailed to do the cooking and Catherine to pluck the birds. Such feverish activity was unusual on the farm with all of them working hard to have everything ready for the first arrivals. Timeliness was of little consequence in the rural areas. Normally what couldn't be achieved in one day could be put off to the morrow. Working under pressure and to a time schedule was a new experience, generating a camaraderie which they all seemed to enjoy.

There was a large turn-out for the event. The MP did not attend but as expected, gave a generous donation and wrote a letter of congratulation to Winstone. Mr Murunga was in his element. He talked at length about Winstone's success in achieving a place in one of the top schools in the country and said it reflected not only Winstone's ability but also the quality of his teaching staff. He urged those of his pupils attending the *harambee* to regard Winstone's achievement as one they should all aspire to. In turn the pastor said Winstone had brought honour to the community and said prayers for his success and well-being at his new school. Lastly Winstone stood up and thanked everybody for helping to provide his school fees and said how grateful he was for their support. Never self-conscious nor lost for words, he gave an eloquent speech which was greeted with a great round of applause.

Towards the end of the afternoon Winstone was beginning to feel uncomfortable. He was not one to relish the limelight. While so much praise had been heaped on him, Absalom had been left unnoticed in the background. So many people wanted to talk to him about his future in Nairobi he had no opportunity to help serve the food or dispense the beer and the soft drinks for the children, as had been planned. That was all left to Absalom. When the food had been served and the children became restless it was Absalom who found skipping ropes for the girls and a football - albeit rags stuffed into a plastic bag and tied round with string - for the boys and amused them until they left for home. Afterwards, when they were clearing up Winstone apologised to Absalom for leaving him to do all the work.

'But it was your day.' his friend said. 'You needed to enjoy it to the full. I enjoyed it too. Serving the food, it was fun meeting so many people I'd not seen before. But I would've been bored standing around afterwards in polite conversation, so I was glad to get away and be with the kids.'

Elias had been on edge throughout the event. He wasn't anxious about entertaining so many people but he was concerned that the *harambee* would not raise enough school fees for his grandson. When Winstone had read him the letter offering him a place at the school, Elias had been shaken by the fees demanded. Since Winstone had done so well in his entry examination it was imperative he attend the school, but at what cost? Unless the *harambee* yielded a substantial sum of money the only alternative for Elias was to sell some of his land. This he was loth to do. Whereas it was a good fertile area with adequate rainfall, land values were low on account of the distance from the main produce markets. He would have to sell off a large area to meet three or four years of schooling and even then, there was no guarantee he would find a buyer.

It was a tense moment that evening when they sat around the table in Elias's house and began to count the proceeds. The first thing Elias did was to open the envelope from the MP. That gave him some encouragement. It contained a sizeable sum of money, rather more than he had reckoned on.

Seeing the look of surprise on his father's face Crispin commented, 'MPs are well paid Dad and a man in his position, no doubt with children in similar schools, will have a very good idea how much fees are in national schools. He probably recognises too that as a small farmer your income will be limited. From the tone of the letter he wrote to Winstone, he seemed delighted that a boy from this remote and impecunious community has made it to a top-grade school in Nairobi, and that's why I think he's been so generous.'

Since few people in the community had a bank account, there were no cheques. All the money was either in notes or coins and took a long time to count. The notes were carefully piled on one side separated into their various dominations while the coins were stacked according to their value. Winstone had been touched that his close friends, Andrew, Seth, Kelvin and Hillary had all donated to the *harambee* the few coins they had from their savings. Although the amount was small, he appreciated the gesture. When all the money was counted there was a sigh of relief. The *harambee*, which included the family's own contribution, had raised enough for Winstone's first two terms and a sizeable amount for the third term. Elias was pleased with the result. The *harambee* had been very worthwhile. Even so he was uneasy about the shortfall for the third term. God willing, he thought, the money will be found from somewhere. How the fees for the three remaining years would be acquired was a matter of conjecture. With the input of both Crispin and Matthew, Elias hoped the farm would become more profitable. Catherine had agreed to contribute a regular amount from her salary each year and John, with his well-paid job had promised to contribute the lion's share.

Now that attendance at his new school was a reality Winstone thought of the prospect with both elation and apprehension. Elation because of the new experiences it would bring him, new opportunities, a chance to be himself, to grow in knowledge and self-confidence, apprehension because of his participation in a totally new way of living, away from the confines of the small, isolated world in which he had grown up to the enormity of city life which he could hardly comprehend. Here he had grown up with school friends he had known from an early age. They knew each other intimately, their characters, their strengths, their weaknesses. His community and its surrounding area, was the sum total of his experience of life. How easily would he integrate with school mates who were total strangers and came from a variety of different tribes and traditions and would have grown up with experiences very different from his own? How would they regard a boy from one of the poorest communities in the country with such a limited knowledge and experience of the world about him? It was this aspect of his new life that worried him most. Would there be any other pupil with a similar background to his in whom he could confide, or would he be alone and on his own, the poorest of all the boys attending such a prestigious school?

CHAPTER TWELVE

Nairobi was an enigma to most people living in Winstone's community. Those who owned a radio knew that broadcasts came from there. They knew too that the president lived there and that it was the home of the Kenyan parliament, but few could conceive of what life was like in an urban metropolis. John and Crispin were exceptions. John had driven there several times on business and much of Crispin's work had taken him to the city. Winstone would not have been capable of arriving at his new school by himself. He would have been bewildered in an environment so unlike the one he was used to. Starting school in the capital for the first time was a formidable problem for any youngster from the more remote parts of the country. Although Winstone lived a day's bus ride away, for others in the north it could take a couple of days or more and sometimes they came from communities where hardly a soul except a schoolteacher could point to Nairobi on a map. It was not just a matter of knowing where Nairobi was; there was the matter of changing busses and once in such unfamiliar surroundings, actually finding the way to the school itself.

It was a blessing therefore that John, realising the difficulties Winstone would face if he went on his own, offered to drive him there for the start of his first term. Once used to city life he would thereafter travel by himself using public transport.

'Dad,' John had said, 'I think Winstone should spend a few days with us before we leave on our journey. Living in a city will be an entirely new experience for him. A few days in Eldoret, small though it is in comparison to Nairobi, will at least help him to come to terms with urban living.'

Elias agreed. Winstone had been on day trips to Bungoma but had never gone further afield. Bungoma was relatively near and a comparatively small town compared with Eldoret. For Winstone, the opportunity to spend time with John's family in their own home was an exciting prospect.

John lived on a modern estate in a house with a small garden in front and a yard behind. It was the first time Winstone had seen mown grass and trimmed hedges. He was fascinated by taps, hot water coming out of one, cold out of the other. There was a large plastic bowl in the bathroom and when he bathed, he made the mistake of putting the bowl in the bath, filling it with water and then squatting down in the bath and splashing water over his body as he would have done at home. He had no idea you used a plug to fill the bath with water and then bathed in it. Laying in your own dirty water didn't seem right to him. He never imagined it could be hygienic to use a lavatory inside a house. He had to be shown you don't squat on the seat as if you were using a long drop toilet. You sit on it instead. Toilet paper was a novelty too, more comfortable and less troublesome than hunting for leaves.

'They won't provide toilet paper in school,' John had said. 'I'll give you some rolls to take with you.'

It was the first time Winstone had seen a kitchen inside a house. There was no chimney. He wondered how you could make a fire for cooking without using wood until he learnt about bottled gas. A refrigerator was a thing of wonder, but most impressive of all was light in every room at the flick of a switch.

John kept chickens in the yard, but they had little grass and were penned in all day. Winstone wondered what they ate since they couldn't roam and search for their own food, until he realised they were given grain and scraps to eat from the household left-overs. He loved the comfort of the home but with a busy street outside and confined to a small garden he missed the freedom, the space and the peacefulness of the countryside. Life ran at a far faster pace in town than at home and it took him time to adjust to the rush and tear of daytime activities and the overriding need for timeliness. He realised the world of his cousins was so different from his own and he was thankful to have the opportunity to experience this kind of living before attending his new school. The majority of pupils would be from urban environments and he recognised that without the experience of modern living he would become a laughing-stock. The time spent with John's family was no more than the tip of a substantial learning curve for Winstone.

The journey from Eldoret to Nairobi was a revelation, the roller-coaster road rising to great heights and cool air then dropping again to the warmth of lower levels. Winstone had seen hills, but nothing like the inclines he experienced on the journey. Nearing the equator where he expected the temperature to be at its peak the sun began to disappear, and they seemed to be driving through thick smoke. It was cold and people by the roadside selling potatoes were huddled in warm clothes.

Winstone turned to his uncle. 'What's happening? Where's all this smoke coming from?'

John laughed. 'I suppose you haven't seen this before. It's fog. We're up in the clouds.'

'But why are the clouds so low?'

'It's caused by the warm air rising from the Rift Valley and meeting the cold air from the high ground.'

Not long after, they started to descend, the fog cleared, it became warmer, the sun shone and there below them was a magnificent view of the Rift Valley with its lakes far below, shining like jewels in the sun. When they neared the capital towards the end of their journey Winstone remarked he had not realised Kenya was so varied.

'It is one of the most varied countries in the world. Not many lands can boast a tropical coastline, a snow-capped mountain, boiling lakes, deserts, a vast variety of wild animals and a land of forty-odd different peoples,' said John. 'It is as if we have the whole world in our little corner of Africa. I'm really proud to be a Kenyan and to live in such beautiful surroundings. '

'Did the British like Kenya when we were a colony?'

'I suppose they did. It gave them a sort of freedom they didn't have in Europe. But they never really understood us. Their ways were very different from ours. They changed our country completely. We were free roaming pastoralists before the Europeans came. They didn't understand our tribalism. They drew borders round our land and hemmed us in, prevented us from roaming and instead started to develop towns'

'I know. That's why half our people live in Uganda instead of Kenya. One boy at school said the British came to our land uninvited and in return they should let us live in Britain and let us enjoy their standard of living. It's a fair argument but the teacher said he was being disloyal to Kenya. We need all our educated people here to develop Kenya into a prosperous country like Britain.'

'Well the colonial power did leave us with a legal system, a railway, a democracy, agriculture, a world language and an education system. In fact, the prestigious school you are going to now was built by the British, so you can be thankful for that.'

Winstone thought Eldoret was large but he was bewildered by the extent of the capital: the unending shanty towns on the outskirts, imposingly tall buildings in the centre, streets of shops and offices, slums, throngs of people and almost stationery traffic. A shudder went through his body. Nairobi was supposed to be a rich place. In his mind's eye he had thought all the buildings would be new and shiny, the streets clean, the air crisp and fresh, the roads quiet and orderly and that the population would walk slowly and gracefully as they did back at home. Instead, it was almost the opposite. Everywhere there was a restlessness. From the car window what he saw were men with jaded faces, painted complexions of make-up-wearing women, people everywhere bustling from one place to another, the dizzying roar of traffic, drivers irritated by traffic jams and hooting horns, many people walking the streets looking as if they didn't own two Kenyan shillings to rub together, and noise, dirt, pollution and general confusion. For someone from the measured life and tranquillity of a soft and verdant landscape this vibrant city of brittle concrete and tarmac came as a shock. At a crossroads a woman in police uniform put up her hand to stop John while she waved on traffic across his path. John meekly obeyed and drew to a halt. Winstone was amazed. He had not imagined a woman could exercise such power over a man.

Winstone turned and looked at his uncle.

John caught the expression on his face. 'You're surprised a woman is in charge, aren't you?'

Winstone nodded.

'You're going to learn there is a big difference between urban living and tribal life. You know as well as I do that a woman is very much in second place at home. You know that when a group of people are approaching, and you ask how many, we tend to answer, "two men and another person," don't we? We don't even acknowledge the other person is a woman. But in an urban setting we follow European customs and women do wield a degree of power. So, don't be surprised that quite a number of teachers at your school will be women.'

Nairobi was one of the largest commercial and industrial cities south of the Sahara. It was through this city the nation's wealth flowed. Was the sacrifice of living in such conditions worth the wealth that filled the pockets of the richest citizens while those of lesser means drew their living serving those of substance? And how did the wealthy live? Grand houses hidden behind locked gates, guards and watchmen on duty, strands of barbed wire, surveillance cameras, the rich worried their wealth would be looted by gangs roaming the streets. It was only materialism that dragged people into these conditions. Was wealth worth forgoing the peace of the countryside, the simple unhurried way of life, the companionship of a close-knit community, the beauty of nature? Was the stress and strain and insecurity of city living a more satisfying way of life? Money couldn't buy the things Winstone valued most in life. He wondered whether he could survive in such an environment, one so alien to him. His confidence began to wane, the more so when the road leading to the school gates passed through a slum of tents and shacks where unkempt children played in roadside mud, raucous women shouted at one another and men peed in the bushes.

He had to keep a hold of his feelings. He dared not convey his thoughts to his uncle. Winning a place at such a prestigious school was considered by those back at home as a great honour and something his relatives and their neighbours had paid for dearly. Showing a reluctance to live in such an environment would be seen as both an insult and cowardliness. His fate was sealed and Uncle John, unaware of how he felt, drove on relentlessly to the school gates. The watchman at the entrance waved them down checked their credentials and waved them in.

Once inside, all Winstone's misgivings faded. The school was set in an oasis of green. Peace reigned. It seemed like another world; a world not so far removed from the one he had left behind. He was suddenly filled with joy. The city and all its noise and pollution could have been a thousand miles away. The grounds were lightly covered with trees, sunlight filtering through them, dappling the ground in shade. Birds sang above, and branches swayed as monkeys dived from one limb to another. Two lines of mature trees formed an avenue which led to the school. Either side of the avenue, the homes of teachers lay half hidden behind hedges. Beyond the trees were playing fields and beyond them fields with cattle grazing. He could hardly believe such large a slice of open land could be so near the city centre. In the distance he could hear the welcoming buzz of voices.

At the entrance to the main building a group of newcomers were milling around waiting to be greeted by the staff. Employment drew tribespeople to Nairobi from all over Kenya, yet children from only well-off families, mostly resident in the city, could afford to send their children to a school of this calibre. For a while he felt alone until by chance, he came across the only other newcomer from his people. They were immediately glad of each other's company and the privacy afforded them of speaking in a language no one else could share.

Simeon came from Bungoma and as a town dweller was worldly wise. His friendship and his experience came as a relief to Winstone who had yet to come to terms with living in an urban environment. The majority of the new intake of pupils came from the city and by the way they talked about their families and their fathers' jobs it seemed that each one, even at this early stage, was vying for a place in the first- year pecking order. Winstone could tell these were the boys from well-off homes. Listening to their conversations sapped his confidence. They were describing a lifestyle far beyond anything he had experienced. Much of it seemed to be bragging about what their fathers did for a living and how they spent their money, almost as if they were trying to outdo each other. It was an experience he had not met before. Back home in the village everybody was treated as equal. They almost all came from the same background, sons and daughters of subsistence farmers or from equally poor backgrounds. It quickly became evident to him that wealth created divisions in society which was a concept new to him. The sons of airline pilots, politicians, surgeons, civil servants and the richest businessmen looked down on those of lesser wealth – shopkeepers, small traders, schoolteachers, journalists and the like – and they in turn had little regard for pupils from the poorest backgrounds.

The first full day was spent familiarising themselves with the school. The new intake were escorted by senior prefects who showed them round the facilities. The school itself was extensive. There was a parade ground, a large assembly hall, a chapel, a sick bay, a science block, gymnasium and to Winstone's delight, a large and well stocked art room. The dormitories were separated into four blocks and represented the four "houses" in the school. Winstone found himself allocated to the Green House along with Simeon. The House had a poor reputation on the sports field but was noted for the academic abilities of its pupils.

Outside, the sports grounds were extensive. There was also a swimming pool and an archery range and a sizeable allotment where pupils were expected to help cultivate vegetables for the school canteen. Outwardly the school seemed to fulfil everything Winstone desired. He loved the modern school buildings with their concrete floors and their many facilities. They were such a change from his primary school. He joined the chapel choir, discovered he had a good singing voice, learnt to read music and made friends with pupils older than himself. Out of the money raised at the *harambee* he not only came with his school uniform but also bathing trunks and he enjoyed using the swimming pool. He was no sportsman but with practice became good at archery. Best of all he loved to roam around the grounds in the peace of the evenings, wrapped in his own thoughts and savouring the solitude which had been such a feature of his early life back home.

The lessons were hard and the homework extensive, but the teachers were encouraging, and everyone was eager to learn. From the beginning Winstone performed well in almost all subjects and his experience of painting and drawing soon attracted the attention of Mrs. Okomo, the art teacher.

Yet it was his home background that singled out Winstone from the others in their first year at school. Boys from poor families were few and far between. The only other pupil from a poor background in his year was a Maasai. He had walked to school all the way from Narok and slept out in the open at night. He arrived wearing only a wrap round *nanga* but carried money with him enough to purchase a school uniform. A teacher accompanied him to the shops and afterwards showed him how to wear a shirt and put on underpants and shorts. His parents had raised his school fees by selling cattle but he, like Winstone, had no pocket money. The food in the school canteen was meagre and most pupils supplemented their diet by purchasing loaves of bread. This Winstone could not do and often felt pangs of hunger. There was also a school tuck shop from which boys in his dormitory returned with sweets and snacks, luxuries Winstone was unable to enjoy himself. It was blatantly obvious to his school mates that both he and Lepish Sipaya, the Maasai, were from poor backgrounds. Some took advantage of their poverty; others showed their sympathy.

Lepish was tall, sinewy and reserved almost to the point of aloofness. Nobody in the dormitory was going to mess with somebody who looked fit enough to stave off lions. Attention instead centred on Winstone, even on his first night in the dormitory. Bruce Kamau's father was a high-ranking businessman. Bruce himself was a tall, pushy, swaggering over-confident fat-faced boy with a high opinion of himself. Persuasive talk and smarmy ways soon attracted a few admirers who seemed to be in awe of him. Inspired by their support, he acted as if the dormitory was already under his control. They were not slow in figuring-out that Winstone was a relatively meek newcomer unsure of himself in his new surroundings, and they turned on him.

'Where do you come from boy?' Bruce demanded.

'Near Cheptais,' Winstone answered.

'Near Cheptais? Near Cheptais?' Bruce repeated with feigned incredulity. 'You mean that place in outer space, beyond the realms of civilisation? What's a boy like you doing here in the centre of the universe? You've got no right to be here.'

Bruce's followers giggled half-heartedly in support of their leader.

Winstone was not going to be put down. 'This might be the centre of your universe but Cheptais is the centre of mine.'

'Ooo, cheeky boy! Where are your manners?'

'Where are yours?' retorted Winstone.

'What's your name, sonny?'

'Winstone Wamalwa if you want to know'

'Oh, did you hear that, chaps?' Bruce turned to his followers. 'Winstone! What a posh name for somebody from outer space! We'll have to change that. Can't have his airs and graces here, can we?'

A larger group of boys stood around Winstone now. One or two intimidated by Bruce's stance but wanted to be on his side, half laughed.

'Okay then, you can call me what I'm called at home. Call me "Wani" if you like,' Winstone said, lying through his teeth.

'Yeah,' said a few of the others. 'Wani, that will do.'

'Cheers mate,' said Bruce. 'You're Wani from now on! And I don't want any more of your cheek. I can do without that. What does your father do in that Cheptais place anyway? I suppose he's a poor old subsistence farmer spreading muck over the land and scraping a living from the earth.'

'My father is dead.'

Bruce wasn't going to give up and he certainly wasn't going to commiserate. 'What about your mother?'

'She's dead.'

'So, what did she die of?' Bruce persisted.

'I don't know.'

'Why don't you know?'

'She went away before she died, and we don't know where she went to.'

'Oh, you poor little orphan,' said Bruce in mock sympathy. 'Well, you can count on us to look after you properly, you see if we don't.'

As time went on Bruce gathered a small gang around him. Winstone was aware they were out to make trouble. They picked on a number of other boys in the dormitory they took a dislike to, yet it was Winstone they turned on most, perhaps because he was an orphan and had no father to answer for him. He became the butt of their jokes and pranks. He was sickened by it. It seemed as if all the trouble Mark and Matthew had made for him at home was being repeated here in school. He kept clear of Bruce and his followers as much as he could but couldn't escape from them in the dormitory. Some of the boys went home at weekends and came back with tins of goodies to supplement their school meals. They would share them between their favourites and intimidate Winstone by offering him their delicacies then snatching them away again just as his uncles had done. Hardened by the experience of his twin uncles he ignored them. On other occasions Bruce's gang would return to the dormitory early in the afternoon and hide the bedclothes of those they disliked or would place handfuls of grass between the sheets. Some of his school friends got really upset by the teasing and bullying meted out by Bruce and his gang, but Winstone stood firm and refused to be intimidated and that irritated the enemy.

Towards the end of term Bruce gripped Winstone by the shoulder and pointing to his crotch alleged, 'You haven't been cut, have you?'

'What's that to you? It's none of your business.'

'Oh, yes, it is. Didn't I say we would look after you?'

'You don't have to. I can look after myself perfectly well.'

Bruce slapped him on the back of the head. 'Yes or no?'

Winstone stood his ground. "If it matters all that much to you, no, I haven't been circumcised.'

'Fourteen and not been cut yet!' Bruce was mocking him again. 'You get yourself cut before next term or I'll do it for you.' He turned to the rest of the dormitory. 'How many of you have been cut?'

Seeing trouble brewing, most boys put their hands up, whether or not they were telling the truth.

'See! You're in the minority. Scared of the knife, are you? Frightened of the pain, are you? Well, we don't allow cowards in our company. You'd better get it done before next term or as I say, I will do it for you. It'll give me great pleasure. See to it boy!'

CHAPTER THIRTEEN

The school term ended in early April. Winstone and Simeon decided they would travel together to Bungoma. It was a blessing for Winstone since he did not fancy the idea of finding the bus station in the city by himself. Once in Bungoma he would know his way home by local transport.

'Make sure you have a pee before you get on the bus,' Simeon warned. 'It's an all-day journey and there's usually only one toilet stop.'

Once they had settled in their seats, they chewed over the events of their first term at school.

'I hate that Bruce Kamau,' Simeon said. 'He's a fat and arrogant ass. His mates are no better. Interesting isn't it that boys from the richest families are all like that. They think they are better than us just because they've got money. Yet you've only got to look at their exam results. You and I are way better academically than most of them are.'

'Yes, but you know what it's like in the city. It doesn't matter whether they are idiots or not, they'll all get good jobs simply because their fathers know influential people.'

'What are you going to do about circumcision?' Simeon asked.

'I wanted to go through the ritual with my friends last August but Grandfather said he couldn't afford it what with my school fees and uniform and bus fares.

I think I shall have to persuade him to have me done in the clinic or at hospital. He'll have to pay for it, but the cost will be minimal compared with slaughtering an animal and providing all the food and drink that countless people will expect. I'm really cheesed off with that fat ass. If I had my way, I would wait another year, and have it done properly. I would feel a man then instead of sneaking into hospital and having it done behind peoples' backs.'

'I know how you feel,' Simeon said, 'but I reckon there will be all hell to pay if he finds out you haven't been cut. What about that friend who shares your house, has he been done?'

'No, he hasn't. His mother couldn't afford it. Perhaps he and I could have it done together. I'll see what Grandfather says.'

When Winstone arrived home, it was like a hero's welcome. Everyone gathered round the table while Martha served platefuls of food. Within the family Crispin and John were the only people who knew Nairobi but naturally Crispin had not visited Winstone's school and so the questions about his experiences came thick and fast until he was quite exhausted. But he made no mention of Bruce and the trouble he had caused him. That was reserved for the private conversation he had with Absalom while they were getting ready for bed.

'That bastard of a boy called Bruce Kamau really hated me because I had got a place at the school from a poor background. He gave me a hell of a time, and not only me but some of the others he didn't like as well. But it was always me that came off worst. Just because his father was damned rich he thought everyone else was beneath him.'

Absalom was surprised by Winstone's colourful language evidently picked up from school. It was a vocabulary he was not used to.

'You know,' continued Winstone, 'That ass had the cheek to demand I get circumcised before next term.'

'Will you get it done?' asked Absalom.

'I don't know what to do. I don't see why I should obey his orders but if I don't then it's going to be an uncomfortable ride next term.'

'You'd have to get it done in hospital, wouldn't you?'

'Yes, or the clinic.'

'I wouldn't mind being done at the same time. Do you think your grandfather would pay for me as well?'

'We'll ask him tomorrow. We can recuperate together then, but we shall probably have to be in bed for a day or two, so it would mean the others would have to look after us.'

Elias said it was time they were both circumcised and it was better done at the beginning of the holiday so that they would be properly healed before they returned to school. Winstone and Simeon had arranged to travel back to school together. When they met in Bungoma Simeon asked Winstone, 'Well then, did you get cut?'

'Yes, I did.'

'So did I,' said Simeon. 'I wasn't going to risk Bruce and his mates turning on me. Actually, it wasn't as painful as I thought it would be.'

'Grandfather said it depends on one's pain threshold and the attitude of mind. Anyway, I am glad it's over. Just think, we are now regarded as men! What do you say to that?'

The new term started well. Mrs. Okomo was impressed with Winstone's artwork. She had spent time in the holiday buying in an easel and acrylic paints for him to use. Winstone felt honoured when told what she had done.

'I've done the same for one or two gifted students in the past,' she volunteered. 'It's not favouritism; it's in recognition of your talent.'

Meanwhile Bruce was so occupied boasting to his mates how he had spent the holidays that he kept clear of Winstone for the first few days. Winstone was still indignant that Bruce's outburst at the end of the last term had obliged him to be circumcised in hospital rather than going through the rite of passage as was expected in his community. He was worried his mates at home might think that since he was living a privileged life, he was too posh to go through such a ceremony. Worse still, they might believe he had ducked out of the test of manhood because he was a coward. The thought burned his mind that perhaps he was a coward obeying Bruce's demand instead of defying him. What possible explanation could he give them if they asked? If he said he had given in to another boy's threat, he certainly would be regarded as a coward. He realised he had fallen into a trap. Either way he had lost face.

Then late one afternoon after Bruce had spent several days boring his followers with his holiday exploits and was looking for something new to amuse himself, he suddenly rounded on Winstone. The boys had returned from the sports field. They had showered and discarded their sweaty sports clothes and were in the dormitory changing into school uniform.

With a smirk on his face Bruce almost butted Winstone head on and said, 'Well mate did you get yourself cut?'

Winstone was on the defensive. 'What concern is that to you?'

'Didn't I say I would do it for you if you hadn't got it done? That's a generous offer you know.' Bruce was leering at him as he spoke, his fat face a picture of hate.

Winstone had experienced mean and hurtful deeds from his uncles but never raw hate, and that riled him. To his surprise he found himself starting to challenge Bruce. 'So where are you going to carry out the circumcision and where will you get a knife from and what do you think the school will say when they find out? Be practical you idiot, and stop making up stories.'

Winstone faced Bruce defiantly, arms folded across his chest. By now the pair of them had gathered an audience. Tension was rising. It looked as if there might be blows.

Bruce hadn't expected to be challenged and made to look foolish. He dodged the issue by repeating his question. Shouting at Winstone he demanded, 'Did you or did you not get yourself cut? And did you get yourself plastered with flour and covered with mud and did you scream like hell when they cut you with the knife?'

Winstone glared at Bruce and said nothing. Flashed through his mind was Jesus standing silent before Pilate.

'Well answer me, boy!' Bruce was almost spitting in Winstone's face.

'You've got it wrong, Brucie,' someone shouted. 'His people rarely circumcise in November. It's mostly done in August and in any case, it is only done in an even year and this isn't an even year!'

'You don't say,' said Bruce. 'Then the coward must have done it in hospital or else he's lying and hasn't done it at all! Come on, pull his shorts down boys and we'll find out the truth!'

Bruce's mates advanced on Winstone who didn't give up without a struggle. Eventually overpowered, the truth was out. He had been circumcised and presumably done in hospital.

While Winstone was putting himself together again Bruce shouted a tirade of insults. 'You cry baby, you coward, you son of a bitch. You said your mother was dead. You're kidding yourself. She isn't dead. She left you to go after other men. I know her type, you, poor little orphan. You're not an orphan at all. She's alive. She's a whore, that's what she is! She's gone after other men and left you. Fancy having a mother as a whore! You, poor boy.'

His outburst renewed Winstone's sense of cowardice for allowing himself to be circumcised at Bruce's behest. Calling his mother a whore, stung him. Embittered by being exposed to his mates and enemies added to the growing feeling of hate towards his adversary. Hate turned to anger. Anger turned to fury. Fury obliterated reason. With an impulsive rush of adrenalin fury became a raging fireball consuming his emotions, devouring all reason. Gripped in a frenzy, his whole body quivering, his eyes unfocused, he sprang forward and lunged at Bruce, punching him hard in the chest with one fist and an upper cut under the chin with the other. Bruce was caught completely off guard. He staggered helplessly, losing his balance, tried to regain it, tottered for a few moments, fell backwards, crashed against the end of a metal bedstead and collapsed on the floor unconscious. Blood slowly oozed from the back of his head. For a moment you could hear a pin drop. Everybody froze. In those few short moments the events in Winstone's life had changed.

Then someone shouted: "Get the matron! Quick, run for the matron!"

A couple of boys tore out of the room. The rest didn't move. Winstone was shaking violently with an overdose of adrenalin, his skin clammy, his body limp, unsteady. He couldn't comprehend what he had done. He stood staring at Bruce's crumpled body in disbelief.

His mind flashed back to his father lying dead next to where he was to be buried, Mark being lowered into his grave, and Absalom unconscious on the playing field. Frightening though they were, these had been natural occurrences. There was no human intervention. No blood had been spilled. Blood implied force applied to the body, force applied by his own two fists. As he stood there, Bruce lying limp and unmoving on the floor in front of him bleeding, the realisation came to him that he, and he alone, was to blame for felling his enemy.

Simeon was the first to move. He came forward putting an arm round Winstone's shoulders to steady him saying, 'That was incredibly brave of you. No one else dare do such a thing. That arse needed teaching a lesson. He deserved every bit of it.'

Winstone didn't hear him. He was dazed. His mind had switched itself off. Boys were murmuring to each other and staring at Winstone. One whom they thought was a weakling had stunned them with his show of strength. Still nobody moved. The two boys came running back with a stretcher shortly followed by matron. By now Bruce had come around and his eyes were open. Through dazed vision Winstone realised he had not killed Bruce. Yet he knew what he had done would have serious consequences. Violence was not part of his nature. What had caused him to act so uncharacteristically was beyond his imagination.

Winstone was brought quickly back to his senses when the matron shouted at him, 'Wamalwa, you'll be expelled for this! Such behaviour is not tolerated in this school.'

Bruce was lifted onto the stretcher and she and the boys hurried off to the sick bay. The word "expelled" rang in Winstone's ears like a death knell. It signified the end of his education in Nairobi and Bruce, when he had recovered, would have the last laugh. He would see Winstone banished permanently from the school. Cynically he wondered whether this was the outcome Bruce had been working for all along, to see him sent packing once and for all-time to "outer space", the place he believed he should belong. The thought of returning home in disgrace with his hard-won school fees and the communal effort to get him educated, wasted, was more than he could bear.

Simeon made him sit down on his bed and recover while he went off to get a cloth and bucket of water to wash the blood off the floor. By now the dormitory was deserted since everyone had gone for their evening meal. Winstone felt too sick to eat. Simeon sat with him for a while then went off for his meal. He was loath to leave his friend in his condition. On the way back, he stopped at the tuck shop and bought a bottle of drink and a couple of bread rolls and gave them to Winstone. Winstone accepted them meekly.

'I'm ashamed of myself,' Winstone confessed, 'ashamed at what I've done, ashamed that I'll be expelled, ashamed to return home and face all those people who worked so hard and so generously to raise my school fees, ashamed to think of what my parents would have thought of me if they'd been alive, ashamed of hurting someone even though I hated them.'

'But you acted honourably. You defended your mother's name and you've taught a bully a lesson. If Bruce had continued to bully you the way he has without reigning him in you would have been seen as a coward, and that you're certainly not.'Meanwhile, instead of going for his meal Lepish had made for the secretary's office. He had a more urgent matter on his mind than food. His appearance, tall, lean, and manly, always made an impression on the secretary. Normally restrained and composed, she was surprised to see him looking flustered

'Madam,' he said, 'I need to speak to the headmaster urgently.'

'Is something the matter Sipaya?'

'Yes, Madam. It's a personal matter, Madam.'

There was something earnest in his speech. She knew him to be reserved, so it seemed evident his impatience must signify something important.

'Well, the headmaster is on the telephone at the moment. If you'll wait outside, I'll speak to him when he's finished and find out if he'll see you.'

Lepish stood in the corridor. He heard the headmaster put down the receiver and the secretary speaking to him. Then the headmaster called him in. The headmaster was sitting with his back to the window. The setting sun shone full on Lepish as he stood a respectful distance from the headmaster who, for a moment, contemplated the boy's sinewy torso, dark complexion and the large round holes in his earlobes which at home would have held ivory earrings.

'What is it Sipaya?'

'Sir, there has been a fight in our dormitory.'

'I know. I've just been speaking to the matron on the telephone. I gather Wamalwa attacked Kamau and punched him unconscious.'

'Sir, the matron said he would be expelled. With due respect sir, that would be an injustice. With the Maasai people, respect for everyone is paramount no matter who they are or what their age. Sir, society crumbles if individuals are not respected. Respect is the very foundation of society.' He spoke eloquently and with conviction. 'Bruce Kamau has no respect for others, only for himself. He's bullied Wamalwa relentlessly since the beginning of the year simply because he's from a poor background and is an orphan and has no parents to stand up for him. This afternoon he sullied the memory of Wamalwa's mother by declaring her a whore. That was despicable. If someone had said the same about my mother, whether dead or alive I would have treated the accuser in the same way. He also tore down Wamalwa's shorts to see if he was circumcised. Sir, in my humble opinion Kamau is a disgrace to the school.'

There was a pause. 'That boy is not afraid to speak out for what he believes, eloquently too,' the headmaster was thinking. 'And he has a maturity beyond his years. Strange for one from people whom we tend to believe live primitive lives.'

'Those are strong words,' the headmaster commented. 'I hear what you say, Sipaya. Thank you for coming to see me.'

Back in the dormitory that evening the atmosphere was subdued. Bruce was kept in the sick bay for the night. His mates were still coming to terms with what had happened. Winstone himself was in the depths of despair and the rest of the dormitory was wondering what the outcome would be for him.

At breakfast next morning a number of those who were not in Bruce's gang came up to Winstone and congratulated him. Bruce and his followers had induced tension in the dormitory ever since their arrival and the rest of the dormitory had all suffered the effect of his dominance. Yet only Winstone had had the courage to tackle him. For Winstone however it seemed a huge sacrifice if it led to expulsion.

Bruce did not appear for the first lesson of the day. Midway through the lesson a prefect was sent to tell Winstone the headmaster wanted to see him. All eyes were on him as, with a heavy heart, he got up and walked slowly to the door. One or two of the boys murmured "good luck, Wani" as he left the classroom.

When he arrived in the corridor outside the headmaster's study, his heart sank. Bruce was standing there with his head bandaged. They avoided looking at each other. When the headmaster called them in, they stood in silence some distance apart. The headmaster was in no hurry to speak. His silence only emphasised the seriousness of the matter.

'Wamalwa,' he said at last, 'you'll be aware that fighting in school is an offence punishable by expulsion?'

Winstone said nothing.

Turning to Bruce the headmaster said, 'bullying a student continually both orally and physically is mentally as painful as being punched to the ground. Indeed, it can be even more painful because it can last over a period of time. Both of you have acted improperly. By rights you should both be expelled. But since this was mutually bad behaviour, I have decided not to expel you but to punish you both in school. I have asked my secretary to reorganise the school cleaning rota. Starting from tomorrow, you, Wamalwa, will clean daily all the boy's toilets in the school for a whole month. That will necessitate you being out of bed at five in the morning and start cleaning a quarter of an hour later. You, Kamau, will clean daily all the staff toilets, both male and female for a whole month starting tomorrow at the same time in the morning. From now on I expect you to show respect for each other. Any further trouble caused by either of you or indeed anyone else in your dormitory will lead to immediate expulsion. You may go now.'

Outside in the corridor Bruce turned to Winstone and said, 'I'm sorry for the

way I've been treating you.' Winstone said, 'I'm truly sorry I hurt you.'

And they shook hands.

Back in the classroom Winstone's face was expressionless but inside he felt huge relief at the outcome. When the lesson finished the class crowded round him. When he heard Winstone was not going to be expelled Lepish was one of the first to congratulate him.

CHAPTER FOURTEEN

When he returned to school for the third term Winstone
was apprehensive. He carried with him the fees for only
half of the term. Whereas Elias had been convinced
that between them they could raise the shortfall from
the *harambee*, this was not to be. The farm had not
produced as much income as was expected. Crispin
had given most of his savings to help pay for the first
two school terms and whereas Catherine contributed
some of her income, John had nothing to give. Miriam,
his wife, had been ill. She had lost a lot of weight.
Then her eyesight had begun to fail. When she was
finally examined it emerged that she was suffering
from diabetes and needed to inject insulin daily if she
was to live. There was no cure. It came as an enormous
blow to John. He had to pay for extra help in the house
before Miriam's illness was diagnosed. Then the cost
of insulin and associated drugs claimed most of his
spare income and would do so for the foreseeable future.
They had all felt embarrassed sending Winstone back
to school with insufficient fees. They knew the school
would accept less than the full amount so long as the
shortfall was made up during the term and had hoped
to find the money from one source or another by then.

At least there was no more bullying. Bruce had learnt
a lesson from being as near to expulsion as Winstone
had been. He and his mates no longer commanded the
dormitory and peace reigned. This allowed Winstone to

enjoy life at school to the full. Since his voice had not yet broken, he was asked to sing solo in the end-of-term concert. His archery had improved considerably, and he was now taking part in team events. He was near the top of the class in his exams and in the art room he had acquired a sizeable portfolio of his own drawings and paintings. One thing he had not learnt however was the art of drawing portraits. Mrs. Okomo decided to devote the new term to portraiture, not only for Winstone but for the rest of the class. She maintained that if her students were to be good all-round artists, the ability to draw and paint portraits was essential. At first, they learnt to copy photographs by mapping out lightly in pencil the head and shoulder dimensions and gradually filling in the features. Then later in the term students sat as models so that the class could begin to develop three-dimensional concepts.

Winstone was fascinated with this technique and Mrs. Okomo opened up the art room on Saturday afternoons so that he and a few other students had extra time to practice and develop their skills. Additionally, Winstone was asked to join the drama group which was preparing an end-of-term play. Throwing himself in all this activity, Winstone forgot about the shortfall in his school fees. It came as a shock to him when one morning the headmaster called for him to come to his office and broke the news that he would be sent home since the full amount of his fees had not been paid.

'I'm so very sorry', he said. 'You're such a promising pupil Wamalwa. I'm very sad to send you away from school. I'm afraid this means you'll not be able to sit the end of year examinations in which in your teachers' opinion you would do extremely well. Therefore, we'll have no measure of your real ability. If I had my way, I would have made an exception in your case and let you stay to the end of term. However, the school governors are adamant that pupils with outstanding fees be sent home three quarters of the way through the term and although I've spoken to the Chairman he'll not be moved from that decision. Nevertheless, if it's any comfort to you, your place in school will be reserved if your family can raise the fees for next year. I sincerely hope they'll find a way of accomplishing this. My secretary will give you your bus fare and you'll need to leave tomorrow morning.'

Winstone's heart was pounding. In a matter of minutes his world had collapsed. His education at the school seemed doomed. He knew the family were relying on John to find the lion's share of his school fees in subsequent years. Now with Miriam's illness and the continued cost of medication that was no longer an option. Being immersed in activities, Winstone had dismissed the matter of school fees from his mind. He had after all jumped his biggest hurdle by winning a place at a school few from more prosperous walks of life could aspire to since they lacked academic ability. Not only had he made the grade, he was excelling in his schoolwork. It might have been presumptuous of him, but he believed he was destined for a bright future. Indeed, he was convinced he deserved it. Mingling with pupils whose parents could well afford to send their sons to one of the nation's top educational establishments he was no longer mindful of his poor background and had pushed aside the fact his family no longer had the means to pay his fees.

Winstone stared blankly at the headmaster not knowing what to say. It meant he would not sing in the chapel choir. He would not perform in the end of

term play. Worst of all, the joy of using the facilities of
the art room, had come to an abrupt end.

'I can see it has come as a shock to you.' The
headmaster spoke kindly. 'Let's hope you will be back
with us next term.' He got up from his desk and shook
Winstone's hand. It was a firm, warm grip.

Winstone mustered just enough strength to say, 'Yes,
sir. Thank-you sir,' as the headmaster opened the door
for him and watched him walk away.

Winstone did not go back to his lesson. Instead, he
went out into the school grounds, sat by a tree and
wept. At lunch time he sneaked into the art room and
took his portfolio. He hid it under his bed and while the
dormitory was empty, packed his suitcase. He planned
to leave very early in the morning without telling a
soul about his departure. He attended lessons in the
afternoon but said nothing to anybody. When lessons
were over, he went to the secretary to collect his bus
fare.

'We're so sorry to see you leave,' she said, handing
over the money. 'It's such a shame, a bright pupil like
you.' She put her hand on his shoulder. 'Let's hope you'll
be back next year. And oh, by the way, Mrs. Okomo
would like you to see her before you leave. She's waiting
for you in the art room.'

Mrs. Okomo was sitting at her desk looking somewhat
concerned. She got up, drew up a chair for Winstone
and sat down again. She motioned Winstone to sit.

'Wamalwa, my star pupil,' she began. 'It's come as
such a shock. I had no idea your fees had not been paid.
I've only heard about it today. You're one of the best
pupils I've had. I'm going to miss you very much. You
must tell me about yourself. You know, although you've
been with us for nearly a year, I really know nothing

about you. They call you Wani don't they? Tell me a bit about your background.'

'I'm an orphan,' Winstone began. 'My parents died when I was still young.'

Mrs. Okomo's expression changed. She was looking at him sympathetically. 'Oh, I'm so sorry to hear that. Was it an accident then?' she said with feeling.

'No. First my father died and then my mother.'

'Do you have any brothers and sisters?'

'No. I'm an only child, Madam'

'Oh, well then, who looks after you?'

'My grandparents, Madam. They brought me up.'

'So, what does your grandfather do?'

'Well, he's just a smallholder really but he has a lot of land and produces good quality food which he sells in the market, but he doesn't make a lot of money out of it. In fact, I wouldn't have been here at all if we hadn't held a *harambee* to raise my school fees.'

'I see. So that explains why you're short of fees. Now I understand. Tell me, at which market is it that he sells his produce?'

'Cheptais market, Madam, just below Mount Elgon.'

'Cheptais?' Mrs. Okomo smiled. 'Oh, I know that area well. I had no idea you came from that far away. You've a long bus journey ahead of you tomorrow. Where abouts is the farm?'

'It's about a twenty-minute walk out of town, to the western side. You can't see it from the road Madam. It's up a long track.'

Mrs. Okomo paused. For a moment her eyebrows knitted in thought as she ran her tongue along her bottom lip. Speaking slowly and thoughtfully she said, 'Tell me, what is your grandfather's name?'

'Wamalwa,' Winstone said, 'like mine.'

'Wamalwa is a very common name in that area. There are so many families named Wamalwa. No, I mean what is his Christian name?'

'Elias, Madam.'

Mrs. Okomo was silent for a moment. Her face stiffened.

'Elias? Did you say Elias?'

'Yes, Madam. Elias Wamalwa, Madam.'

Now Mrs. Okomo looked startled. Winstone wondered whether he had said something wrong.

'Elias Wamalwa?'

'Yes Madam.'

Winstone felt uneasy. She was staring hard at him her expression frozen. He could see tears welling in her eyes. Suddenly she got up from her chair with arms outstretched as if to hug him.

'My son! my son!' she murmured as someone bemused. Then suddenly 'My son! My son!' she screamed.

Winstone was terrified. It was those words again! Avoiding her arms, he scrambled up, knocking over his chair and ran. He ran out of the door as fast as he could. He ran down the corridor without looking back. He ran outside, across the grounds and hid in the trees. Who was this imposter? "My son, my son" had not been said as an endearment. It was more like ownership. The woman he had trusted, who had encouraged him, devoted her time to him, bought in materials to support his artistic ability, was now claiming him as her own. His heart was racing, not just from running but from fear and bewilderment. He thought of the whole of this day with loathing; first his expulsion, then this woman trying to claim him as her son! How could she do such a thing? He wondered about his poor dead mother and

160

what she would have thought of the situation. How he longed to have her hug him now in his deepest distress.

It was cool and peaceful out in the grounds. There were insect sounds and a bird was singing its last song of the day in the tree above. There was no wind. Darkness was falling, and a pale moon was caressed by slow moving clouds. After a while he calmed down and full of resignation, slowly made his way into the dining hall for the evening meal. He didn't join in much of the conversation and afterwards decided not to go to choir practice. After all what was the point? He was not going to be able to sing his solo at the end of term. Instead, he went to the common room and concentrated on his homework, determined to spend every last minute at school on his education.

Next morning, he was up well before the rest of the dormitory, picked up his suitcase and portfolio from under his bed and by the light of a moon, now clear of clouds, crept out of the building.

It was a long walk to the bus station. The air was cold as it often is at that time of day and he turned up the collar of his blazer to keep warm. How he wished he could travel in civvies. Seeing him in his school uniform, people would be wondering what he was doing out of school in term time.

As he neared the city centre, he saw people sleeping in the streets, some in doorways, others just on the pavement snuggled in blankets or sometimes just covered by cardboard in order to stave off the chill air. Some of them were children. When he saw them, some lying in groups, others on their own, he pitied them. Here was he, an orphan but with grandparents to look after him, a roof over his head, food that was plentiful and a school he could go to at home, and these kids had nothing, no certainty in life, no food at hand, no one to hug them, and he felt ashamed, ashamed that he had felt so sorry for himself when there were others far worse off than he was.

He arrived early at the bus station. There were few people around. He sat and waited until the crowds gathered and the busses came in. On the way home a man came and sat next to him and offered him some delicious looking cake. He looked decidedly shady. Winstone did not accept it even though he was hungry. He had heard stories of food offered on busses being drugged. He immediately clasped his portfolio and put his hand on his suitcase. If he had eaten that cake, he might have fallen asleep, only to find when he woke up his suitcase stolen, and his portfolio gone. However, on reaching Bungoma he realised he had more money than he needed to complete his journey and bought himself a loaf of bread.

It was dark by the time he reached home. On the way he decided not to mention to anyone the episode with Mrs. Okomo. For him it was too personal and too distressing. If he seemed depressed to the family, he would simply put it down to his expulsion from school.

Elias and Martha expected the worst when he appeared in the doorway.

'It's happened,' he announced. 'I was expelled today for lack of fees.'

His grandparents looked solemn.

Martha didn't comment. Perhaps to hide her embarrassment she asked, 'Have you eaten today?'

'I bought some bread in Bungoma, but I've had nothing to drink.'

Martha immediately scuttled out to the kitchen to boil tea and prepare a meal, leaving Elias to commiserate.

'Sit and relax,' said Elias. Winstone pulled up a chair and sat down, took off his shoes and put his feet up. It had been a very long day. He had been up at four-thirty in the morning. It had taken three quarters of an hour to walk to the bus station, half an hour to wait for transport in Bungoma, and it was now half-past seven in the evening. He was almost too tired to talk. Elias sat silent, wondering what to say. It was an awkward situation. He couldn't welcome him home because home was not where he should be. He couldn't even ask if he had enjoyed his term a school. Winstone was equally silent. Elias noticed the boy had matured. His face had lost the roundness of childhood and was angular, a prediction of the handsome young man he was to become. He had the features of his father, yet his mouth and his smile reminded him of his mother. The thought of Winstone's parents intensified his sense of failure to provide adequately for their offspring's education. At last he broke the silence.

'I've let you down,' he said. 'In fact, in one way or another we've all let you down, all six of us. Our only grandson and we've failed to raise your fees. It would have been more excusable if there had been five or six grandchildren, but only one grandchild, and a bright one at that and we still couldn't pay your fees.'

'It can't be helped,' said Winstone. 'It wasn't intentional. I know you've always had my best interests at heart. You know, when I walked to the bus station early this morning there were kids sleeping in the street, some of them younger even than me. They have no-one to care for them or feed them or even love them and although I was disappointed at being expelled, I couldn't feel sorry for myself. I have a family to care for me, I have food, I have those that love me and by attending our school here I'll still have an education. I have plenty to be thankful for.'

'I am impressed you think like that,' said Elias. 'It is a measure of your maturity and I admire you for it. But it doesn't ameliorate my view that I've let you down. I think it will always be on my conscience.'

Just at that moment there was a knock on the door and Absalom stepped in.

'Winstone!' he exclaimed, 'how good to see you! I didn't expect you to be home so early. Has term finished already?' They hugged each other.

'No, I ran out of fees and was sent home. I've only just arrived and haven't eaten yet.'

'Does that mean you won't be going back to Nairobi again?'

'I'm afraid not. Next term I shall be joining you at school in Cheptais and you will have to get used to sharing my house with me.'

'That's no problem. I'll enjoy it but I'm really sorry you've been sent home. It must've come as a terrible blow. You must be ever so upset.'

Martha returned with hot food and she served it up while Absalom went to fetch the tea from the kitchen.

'I've put out some food for you as well Absalom,' she called to him. 'I'm sure you can find room for it and you can keep Winstone company.'

After they had eaten the boys went over to Winstone's house.

'You must be pretty tired,' Absalom said.

'Yes, I was up at four thirty this morning, but let's talk. I can sleep in tomorrow morning and that'll be a luxury!'

'What did your classmates say when they knew you were being sent home?'

'I didn't tell anybody after I had seen the headmaster. They will have begun to wonder when they woke up this morning and found I've gone.'

'My father died when you were away. It was alcohol poisoning that took him.'

'Gosh, I'm sorry hear that. He wasn't all that old, was he? It must've been tough on your mother.'

'I'm not so sure about that. In some ways it came as a relief. It put an end to the quarrelling over money. All my brothers and sisters attended the funeral. Some of the older ones I hardly knew. They'd kept away from home because of the attitude of my father. She was really happy to have all the family around her. She's a changed woman, so much more relaxed. She dresses much better as well and she's eternally grateful to Crispin and your grandfather for letting her run the market stall. They've worked out a good scheme. She buys the produce from them. Crispin runs it to the market and then she sells it at a profit and gets a good income. The goods are always fresh, she's a good saleswoman and pleasant to her customers and they flock to her. And by the way, since I no longer have to look after Ellen, now she's older, I work longer hours on the farm and your grandfather pays me pocket money. I'm starting to save to build my own home on our land so that, if and when I get married, I'll have a home to take my bride to. So how was your time at school?'

'It was really great while I was there. Everybody in our dormitory gets on well together now. I was in the chapel choir and the drama group and I've done pretty well at archery.'

'So, you won't be in the end-of-year performances then?'

165

'No. They'll have to manage without me but it's no matter. Oh, and we studied portraiture in art classes this term. It was new to me. I think I got on quite well. We learnt the trick of using triangles to get body proportions right.'

'We don't do so much practical art at our school. It concentrates more on the history of art. Our teacher says that Europeans paint a lot of nude portraits of women. I bet you haven't done any nude ones, have you?'

'Fat chance in a boy's school!'

'There's a girl I know who's a real wow, but unfortunately she doesn't have much interest in me. I would pay you handsomely if you painted a nude portrait of her, you know.'

'Absalom, you have a dirty mind!'

'Not at all. It's the call of nature, isn't it?'

'Anyway, it wouldn't work. My hand would shake too much when I came to paint her private parts!'

'Ha, ha! Now who's got a dirty mind?'

'It's not me! It's that little fellow below. He's always on the rampage. He's the one with the dirty mind and I have a devil of a job reining him in. By the way, have you heard that joke about the woman caught soliciting in the street?'

'No.'

'When she was brought before the judge, he asked the good woman what she did for a living.

"Demolition, sir," she said proudly.

'Demolition?' said the judge. 'That's an unusual job for a woman! What kind of demolition is it?'

"Demolition of temporary erections, sir."

Absalom sniggered. 'For goodness sake, who told you that one?'

'A boy at school.'

CHAPTER FIFTEEN

While Absalom was at school Winstone spent the mornings working on the farm. The early afternoon was spent painting and drawing and when Absalom returned from school, he had a meal ready for him before they both set off to work on the fields.

'I see you've been pinching straws from the kitchen roof to light the fire, just like women do,' observed Winstone.

'Yes, I have,' confessed Absalom. 'It's not really laziness. It's just there is so little time when I've finished on the land and straw lights a fire so much quicker than using wood.'

'I'll forgive you. In fact, the whole roof is dilapidated and will have to be replaced soon. Have you seen how the termites are destroying the woodwork in the house? That too will have to be replaced before long. Isn't it strange? Everything around us is changing all the time. Some things change slowly. We're born young and we die old. A roof is new and after a time it deteriorates and has to be replaced. More alarming are the things that change fast. A tree is standing tall, blasted by lightning and moments later it is split in two and lying on the ground. I'm away at school one day and find myself at home the next. One day my father was alive and the next he was dead. One moment you were running around the playground and the next moment you were unconscious on the ground. Life is so unpredictable.

You never really know what's going to happen next. You can't plan for anything with certainty. You just have to take every day as it comes. Wouldn't it be good if we could foretell the future? Then we would be able to avoid the things in life we didn't like.'

'I don't think that's a good idea. You can never avoid death and if I knew in advance when I was going to die, I'd spend all my time worrying about it.'

'Well, if Mark knew he would be struck by lightning in that storm he could have avoided death by taking shelter indoors.'

'Oh yes? And we would still have had the two of them knocking around and making life difficult for us. No, I think it's better for us not to know the future. It's for our own good.'

John came on a visit with his family shortly after the school holidays had started. Miriam's health had improved once she was injecting insulin regularly.

'It happened so swiftly,' she said. 'One week I was healthy and the next week I was really ill.'

She showed them the needle she had to inject with. Absalom shuddered at the thought.

'You mean you have to put that into your skin several times a day? I think I'd rather die.'

'I don't think you would,' said Miriam. 'If it was a matter of life and death you would do it. And if you were a mother or father you would do it for the sake of your children even though the medication costs a great deal of money.'

'There you are,' Absalom said afterwards. 'If Miriam knew she was going to get diabetes, tell me, what could she have done to avoid it?'

'Okay, Absalom. I give in. I grant you've won the argument.'

To Winstone's surprise Catherine turned up at the week-end unannounced. Winstone and Absalom were at home when John, Catherine, Crispin and Matthew all arrived together on the doorstep.

'We've come with something for you,' they said in unison.

The boys wondered why they had come all together. What was going on?

'Winstone,' John said. 'We're desperately sorry we couldn't pay all your school fees. You must be missing school very much and especially your art classes and the teacher so kind in encouraging you. We wanted you to know we feel for you and although we don't have the means of returning you to Nairobi, the four of us have clubbed together to try to compensate you as best we can.'

While John was speaking Catherine slipped outside and came in with three parcels neatly wrapped in newspaper. One was very large and flat, another smaller and bulky and a still smaller one which was less bulky.

'These parcels are for you, Winstone. We hope you enjoy using them,' said Catherine with a smile.

Winstone thanked her as she handed them over. Turning to Absalom he said, 'Come on and help me open them.' Then turning to his uncles and aunt he said, 'I don't think I deserve all this.'

'You most certainly do,' said Crispin.

Winstone was very surprised when all the parcels had been opened. There was an easel, some canvasses, both of which must have been bought at some cost, acrylic paints and a book called "Improving the Way you Paint". Winstone shook hands and thanked each of them and gave his aunt a hug.

'There,' exclaimed Absalom. 'What were you telling me a week or two ago? You can never predict what is going to happen from one day to the next. Now you can paint that portrait for me. You've got all the equipment you need!'

'Portrait? What portrait is that?' asked Matthew.

'Oh, don't take any notice of him,' replied Winstone. 'It's just a sick joke.'

§

One day in mid-December Elias cycled back from Cheptais with his newspaper and a letter he found in his post box. It wasn't a letter he had expected. It had a Nairobi post mark. He didn't know of anybody likely to send him a letter from there. When he got home and opened it, he thought he recognised the headed paper. It looked as if it was from Winstone's school, but he couldn't be sure.

'I've got this letter,' he said to Winstone, 'and I can't understand it because it's written in English. Will you read it to me please?'

Winstone picked up the letter.

'It's from the headmaster,' he said. 'I wonder why he's written to you? Perhaps it's an apology for sending me home.'

He began reading.

'It says,' *"Dear Mr. Wamalwa. Concerning Winstone Wamalwa. As you will know we were obliged to send your grandson home from school in November because of the shortfall in fees for last term. It is the Governors' requirement that fees should be paid in full well before the end of term. We were very sorry to lose Wamalwa who is an outstanding pupil and would have had a bright future ahead of him.*

However, it gives me great pleasure in writing to you to say...." Winstone faltered. He was pursing his lips and his face puckered. *"in writing to you to say...."* His voice was quivering.

'Well go on boy, what does he say?'

Winstone didn't answer. The words were choking him. He tried again. *"in writing to you to say that an anonymous donor...'*

'Boy, what is it? What's the matter?'

'... that an anonymous donor, possibly an American, has paid your grandson's fees for the whole of next year."

By now tears were rolling down Winstone's cheeks. He read on. *"Term begins on 4th January. He should report to my secretary on arrival. We look forward very much to see him back with us.'*

'Oh, my boy!' exclaimed Grandfather as he clamped his arms round Winstone and hugged him. 'My boy this is the best news I could ever have wished for! This is the answer to my prayers. This is Divine intervention!'

'I apologise for crying, Grandfather. Now that I'm a man I know I shouldn't cry. I'm not crying in pain, nor in disappointment, nor in anger, but in joy. Is it taboo to cry in joy?'

'Certainly not. You have good reason to cry for joy. It's an expression of your gratefulness to God that he's sent someone with compassion to send you back to your school. This is extraordinary. Who do you think the donor could be?'

'I don't know,' said Winstone, drying his eyes. 'If it is anonymous, it can't be anybody from school. There are several boys from rich families in my class, but I don't think it would be any of them. It seems to me most rich people are reluctant to part with their money. That's why they get rich. I can only think of Simeon, my best friend at school, but his parents struggle to pay his fees, so it can't be them. It's a mystery to me, but I'm so grateful whoever it is.'

In some respects, the letter, despite its promise, had unsettled him. He wondered about the authenticity of the American. Coming from his remote village he had not seen a white man until he went to Eldoret, so why should an American want to support a coloured boy whom he didn't know and had never met? While the letter confirmed that his fees had been paid for the coming year, what would happen after that? He had heard of many kids from his poverty-stricken area who had been thrown out of school because a promised gift of money had dried up. They had left their homes resplendent in new school uniforms, fired with enthusiasm for all the benefits education would bring them, only to return home a year or two later, downcast and disconsolate when their dreams had turned to ashes. These children were not attending an up-market national school but local secondary schools where the fees were modest. For them the aspiration of a good education with long term prospects of obtaining a job and a salary substantial enough not only for their own needs, but to enable them to send money home to raise their parents above the poverty line were dashed, and the prospect of becoming a mere subsistence farmer loomed large.

While Winstone was pleased and relieved to continue his education in Nairobi, at least for the foreseeable future, a dark cloud hung over the time he would spend there. It was the thing to do with Mrs. Okomo. After he arrived home, he had quickly dismissed the incident, believing by not going back to that school it was of little consequence. Now it plagued him again. Was there really any significance in the incident? Were there two Elias Wamalwas living near Cheptais? Could she have mistaken him for somebody in another family? Was there still a possibility his mother was alive? Mrs Okomo was an artist like his mother, but her surname was from the Luo tribe and not his own people. The Luos occupied the land along the shores of Lake Victoria. They were fine musicians and their origins were Nilotic, not Bantu as he was. She didn't exactly look like a Luo. Could it be that his mother had remarried? Mrs. Okomo had never mentioned being married or having a family. It bothered him that he couldn't recall his mother's face. He couldn't say he recognised any likeness in Mrs. Okomo. Then again, she seemed older than his mother would have been. Or were her words really meant as an endearment and was it because she was overwrought as a result of her star pupil being sent home? That might have led her to sound as if she possessed him.

Winstone's torment was all the greater in that he couldn't express his doubts to anyone. There were barely three weeks left before the start of term and he needed to search for a means of handling a matter that now began to occupy all his thoughts. Somehow, he needed to devise a plan that would settle once and for all whether or not Mrs. Okomo could be his mother.

After many days of soul searching a tentative plan formed in Winstone's mind. There was however a risk attached to it and he wasn't sure whether or not he should pursue it. It involved his mother's head scarf. He could give it to Mrs. Okomo as a present. If she recognised it, she would be his mother; if she didn't recognise the scarf, she wouldn't be his mother and he would have lost a precious memento of her, one that meant so much to him. He went to the wardrobe, took out the scarf and held it in his hands. He hesitated. Dare he take the risk of losing it? It still held an aroma of the scent his mother used to wear. He looked back at the wardrobe. Two dresses still hung there. He would rather have lost one of those, but it would be too ostentatious to give Mrs. Okomo a dress. Yet the headscarf was more dear to him than the dresses since his mother wore it almost every day and he associated her more closely with the scarf than the dresses. He stood there for a long time, wondering what to do. What else could he give Mrs. Okomo that would test whether or not she was his mother? One of her paintings or drawings might have been appropriate if his teacher hadn't been an artist herself. The only other item he could think of was his father's club, but it would be unseemly to give a club as a gift. It seemed there was no alternative. He was resigned to using the scarf.

Then another dilemma confronted him. If Mrs. Okomo was not his mother, he couldn't give her something that smelt of being used by another person. That meant he would have to wash the scarf to remove the perfume that meant so much to him. When no one else was around he went into his kitchen, heated some water, got some soap and with a heavy heart washed the scarf. He hated what he was doing. It was as if he was washing away the memories of his mother; being disloyal to his remembrance of her. When it was washed, he put it out to dry in the sun. Then when it had dried, he took his mother's box iron, filled it with hot ashes and ironed the scarf. He folded it carefully then went to the drawer where the paintings were kept and took out the carefully preserved wrapping paper his aunt Catherine had put round his presents in all those years ago.

At the beginning of his second year at national school he left for Nairobi not knowing what his fate would be. He tried to prepare himself for both scenarios, life without a mother and life with a mother. It was difficult not to be emotional about his future. He tried to put it out of his mind and concentrated instead on thinking what it was he wanted to draw and paint in the year ahead of him.

CHAPTER SIXTEEN

Winstone went directly to the secretary's office when he arrived at school. The secretary got up to greet him. She was a kindly, motherly woman, dedicated to her job and to the pupils who came to her for help and advice when they were in any kind of difficulty and although it was not her responsibly, she spent much of her time mentoring those in trouble.

'It's so good to see you again,' she beamed. 'Welcome back! Your year's fees have been safely paid into the bank, so you can settle down to your studies without that worry at the back of your mind. We still have no idea who the donor is. We suspect it might be a well-off American who has heard of your case. We have had one or two old boys from the United States visit the school recently. Whoever it was has also realised you need more than your fees. He has left you a generous amount of pocket money. I've opened an account for you, and I have prepared a pocket money book in which I shall record how much you withdraw and record how much is left. The headmaster has asked to see you as soon as you arrive. I don't think he has anybody in with him at the moment, so you can go and knock on his door. Oh, and by the way, Mrs. Okomo has asked to see you. She would like you to call at her bungalow before you take your meal in the dining hall this evening.'

He went to see the headmaster. They shook hands and he welcomed Winstone back to school.

'Your donor remains a mystery.' he confessed. 'I just hope he will support you for a further two years until you finish school here. He is obviously a very generous man.'

While he was settling into school several of his classmates expressed surprise and delight that he was back with them.

'We wondered what had happened to you when we found your bed empty and your suitcase gone,' Simeon said. 'We wondered whether you'd been kidnapped until word leaked out you were short of fees and you were sent home.'

'I was too ashamed to admit to it,' Winstone confessed. 'That's why I left without telling anybody.'

One of the choirboys volunteered: 'It wasn't the same without you at the end of term concert Wani. We missed the clarity of your voice.'

That cheered Winstone a bit since the impending visit to Mrs. Okomo was weighing heavily on his mind. What should he do if, when he knocked on her door, she greeted him by flinging her arms around him and called him her son? The thought horrified him. He would have nowhere to hide the present he was carrying. If he gave her the scarf it would seem as if he was condoning her action. Then again, if she did try falsely claiming to be his mother how could he get out of the situation? It would be the ruination of his relationship with her as a teacher. He would have to go to the headmaster, or better still the secretary and ask her to sort things out. It was ironic that he so badly wanted to be at this school yet faced with this situation he was beginning to think it would have been better to continue his education back home.

It was a dark and dreary day with clouds gathering, rain promising, and the light fading as he made his way to Mrs. Okomo's home. The weather heightened his sense of foreboding. When he reached the gate, he feared opening it. There was a neatly cut hedge separating the garden from the lane he had walked along. Inside it was mostly grass with one or two shrubs and large poinsettias on either side of the porch. It was in a wooded area with mature trees overhanging both sides of the garden adding to the gloom, a gloom which at this moment in time entombed his soul, his mind and his willpower. It would be only a matter of minutes before he knew the thing that had been such a burden for most of his life. One that mattered to him more than anything else. Was his mother alive or was she not? When a child is parted from its mother suddenly, without reason and without explanation, it must always leave behind in the child's mind a sense of insecurity, of longing, and a heartache which gnaws away at the soul until closure is found. Winstone sensed that closure was near at hand, but he dared not anticipate the outcome. He stood by the gate for a moment then walked on a few steps paused and then walked back. He still couldn't face opening the gate. The porch light was on so Mrs. Okomo was obviously expecting a visitor. He walked by then turned again. Something inside him was insistent. He must go on. He must go through with it. His heart was racing, sweat under his arms, hands clammy. Suppressing his fear, he pushed open the gate and made his way to the front door. He knocked. It was a solid door, but he knew Mrs. Okomo was coming to open it because he saw a shadow pass by the lit living room window. He held his breath, his heart still racing. The door opened and Mrs. Okomo stood there very calm and serene.

'Come in Wamalwa,' she said. 'Welcome back. I'm so pleased to see you. Do come in.'

Winstone walked into the well-lit room. It was decorated quite differently from other teachers' homes he had visited. There was a lampshade on the ceiling light rather than just a bare bulb. The walls, instead of being bare and coloured with the usual cream with green woodwork, were painted dove grey and covered with pictures. In the middle of the room stood a coffee table, dressed with a small cloth, and a vase of flowers. Two armchairs and a settee were set around it. At the far side of the room stood a dining table and four chairs. The table was set for a meal for two. There was an electric fire with a mantlepiece above, and a clock.

'Thank you,' he said. 'Yes, it's good to be back.' He hoped she didn't notice the quiver in his voice

'I have to apologise to you. I shouldn't have acted in the way I did and said the things I did when you left last term. I was so overwrought at the thought of losing my best pupil, one who has so much talent. I hope you'll forgive me.'

'Then she's not my mother after all,' thought Winstone, 'otherwise she wouldn't be making an apology. Nor would she be so formal.'

The spark of hope faded within him. He was loath to give her his parcel, but he had it in his hand and it was obvious it was something he had brought for her.

'Yes, of course. It's kind of you to invite me to your house. I...I've brought you a small present.' He was doing his best to remain positive and bury his misgivings.

'Oh, that's very kind of you,' Mrs. Okomo said in a tone of surprise. 'But you needn't have done that.' She took it from him gracefully. 'May I open it now?'

Winstone bit his lip, hesitated for a moment then said, 'Yes.'

'It's very beautiful paper and neatly wrapped too with the same care and attention you apply to your paintings.'

They were still standing at the entrance to the room. Winstone wished he didn't have to watch her opening his parcel, but it would have been rude to look away. She took the string off very carefully and slowly unwrapped the paper. The yellow fabric came into view. She was staring at the scarf still holding it in the wrapping. Winstone's nerves were on edge. He turned away for a moment not daring to see her reaction. His chest was tight. He could hardly breathe. He turned back. The moment of reckoning had come. It seemed as if she stood there for an age, captivated by what she was holding in her hands, hardly able to assimilate what it was she was seeing.

Then she looked up at him, tears welling in her eyes.

'My scarf,' she murmured. Then, 'my yellow scarf!' she exclaimed. 'It's my yellow scarf!' Tears were streaming down her face. 'Oh, Wanyonyi, Wanyonyi, my son!' and she flung her arms round him. Winstone was crying floods of tears now as they embraced each other.

'Mama, oh Mama, how I have missed you all these years. I thought I would never find you. I thought you were dead!'

They hugged each other for a long time, she stroking his head, both crying on each other's shoulders just as they had done when Papa had died.

Eventually he said, 'I seem to have spent so much time in my life crying. Crying for Papa, crying for you, crying even when my school fees were paid and now crying with you. I felt ashamed if I cried after I was circumcised but Grandfather said it was alright to cry if one was crying for joy.'

'I cried a lot too, crying when Papa died and crying for you when I left you. It was the hardest thing I've done in my life. I was sick with sorrow. I was heartbroken.'

'But Mama, why oh why did you leave me when you loved me so much? It didn't make sense to me. One minute you were loving me intensely and the next moment you'd gone. I couldn't understand it. It was all so sudden.'

They were drying their eyes and standing apart again.

'I know, it must've been really awful for you. More awful even than it was for me. I grieved for you intensely for months afterwards. You were my only link with your dear father. Without you I felt bereft, so utterly lonely, so desolate. But did your grandparents never tell you why I left? Why I had to run away so suddenly? Have they never explained the situation to you? You were too young to understand at the time, but later I mean?'

'But what situation Mum? What made you run away so suddenly? What could ever have made you leave me? I just don't understand.'

'You didn't know then that among our people when a husband dies, a younger brother of the husband is entitled to inherit his widow and make her his wife? Didn't you know that? Didn't anybody ever tell you that? Didn't they tell you about our custom?'

'No, they didn't. I had no idea! All that Grandmother and Grandfather said was that you had gone away and died. They didn't explain anything else. Not a thing. I would've understood if they'd told me. But you didn't die so why did they keep telling me that?'

'I suppose they thought it would bring closure to my going. They probably thought that if they said I was dead you wouldn't keep grieving for me. My poor boy! You must have suffered terribly. If they'd told you that, you wouldn't have worried that I was dead. You would've known that sometime in the future there was a chance of us being reunited'

'Then is that why there was that terrible row in the house when Mark and Matthew came around one night after Papa died?'

'You remember that do you, even though you were so young? Yes, they came to claim me. It was a horrible situation. I had to defend myself. I beat them with your father's club. I hurt one of them quite badly on the leg. I drove them out the door and that one went off limping. I realised I had to go that night otherwise they would've been back again. I was helpless. I felt absolutely terrible leaving you like that. Indescribable. And I couldn't take you with me because as you know, you belong to your father's family and it's taboo for the mother to take a child away. Had I done so they would have searched and searched until they found me. Besides a mother and child on their own would have raised all kinds of questions and we would both have been very vulnerable to illicit men. I felt my whole family had fallen apart. It was so sudden. There we were, a close-knit family one week and a family no longer the next. My whole world had fallen apart, just as yours had. I cried so much after I left you, but I had no alternative. I think the grief aged me quite a lot.

Just imagine if I had been married to one of those twins against my will. Life would have been hell with them. I just couldn't have lived with them. And suppose they had given me children. How would they have treated you? Your life would have been hell as well because although I was you mother, you know that men have the last say and I would have had no control over what they did to you. That was uppermost in my mind when I left you. I thought you would be much safer under your grandparent's care than being subject to your uncles if I had married one of them. It was the only crumb of comfort I had.'

'As it was, those uncles made my life a misery, taunted me, hit me, hurt me and made me very afraid of them. They did it when they knew grandfather and grandmother were not around and of course they knew very well I had no parents to defend me.'

'Oh Wanyonyi, how terrible. It makes me feel so guilty.'

'No matter, it's all in the past. My uncles are no longer a problem now. You see Mark died and Matthew has changed completely.'

'No!'

'Yes. Five or six years ago you may have heard there was a long drought in our area. The drought was broken by a violent thunderstorm. Matthew said Mark refused to take shelter. There was a bit of an altercation, he told his brother he was a coward for taking cover and insisted on sheltering under the old sycamore fig. The fig was struck by lightning and so was Mark and it killed him. Matthew was devastated. He hid away in his house for quite a long time. He quite changed character. After the funeral he came and begged me to forgive him and his brother for the way they'd treated me. Imagine, a grown man asking a mere boy for forgiveness. I couldn't have coped with the situation if Absalom hadn't been with me. He's been such a good friend.'

'Absalom? But come along, let's sit down. There's lots to talk about. We can take our time. You don't need to go to the dining hall this evening. I've got a meal ready for us.'

Winstone filled in his mother with all the events that had happened during his childhood including his friendship with Absalom right up until he came to be at school in Nairobi.

'Absalom and I are the very best of friends. He helped me overcome the void of having no parents around. We've no secrets between us. We share everything. In fact, it's almost like being twins.'

Delia served the meal she had prepared.

'But Mum, why did you prepare a meal for us? Were you convinced I was your son?'

'When you said where you came from and who your grandfather was on that last day at school, I was convinced you were my son. Then when you got up and ran, I had serious doubts. I thought there were perhaps two Elias's in the area with the same surname. It's sad I didn't really recognise you. I remember you as a small child, but of course you've changed completely since that time. There were occasions in class when I looked at you and thought there were similarities between you and Papa, but I dismissed the idea because your school friends called you Wani and not Winstone and of course Wamalwa as a surname is not uncommon. Then again, I would never have imagined such a remarkable coincidence that you would turn up at the very same school at which I was a teacher.'

'Yes, and the reason why I ran is because Grandmother and Grandfather kept saying you'd died. Then early on I couldn't remember your face. I remembered Papa's very well, but I think it was the shock of you leaving that erased your likeness from my memory. Also, as Mrs. Okomo, I felt you couldn't possibly be my mother, not unless you had married a Luo. I was shocked out of my wits when you said I was your son. I thought you were an imposter or even some sort of ghost from the past.'

'So that's why you brought me my scarf. It was a test to see whether or not I was your mother?'

'Exactly.'

'Amazing!'

'Yes, but it took a lot of courage. That scarf was very dear to me. It was the one thing you always wore, and it smelt of the scent you used. It was the closest reminder I had of you and I was so worried that if you turned out not to be my mother, I would have given away the dearest thing I had of you. Also, I was worried you would insist I was your son when in fact I wasn't. You see, you never wear that scent in school. Had you done so I might have guessed who you were.'

'Yes, of course. But wearing scent in school is frowned upon here.'

'And you see, what's been worrying me most is that you've remarried, and I don't know who your husband is and whether you have some children besides me.'

'Let me reassure you, I never remarried. There's no one who could replace Papa. You see, it was a very difficult time for me. My family never wanted me to marry your father. That's why they didn't come to your christening or your father's funeral. I knew I wouldn't have been accepted if I'd gone back to them and if I'd done so they would've sent me straight back to your uncles. I had to make a new life for myself away from our people and that is why I chose a Luo name as a disguise. All the time I've been at this school I've had to pretend Mr. Okomo was dead, not that there's ever been one in my life. I also had to pretend I had no children, and that was the hardest thing of all. It made me feel as if I was denying your existence. Life was tough to begin with. I went to Naivasha and got a menial job there and lived in little more than a hovel. Then I moved on to Nairobi and got a better job. All the time I was saving as much as I could to pay for the fees to go to university. After I graduated, I obtained a post as a teacher in a private school in Nairobi, teaching art. But I hated city life. Later on, I saw this school was advertising for an art teacher. I was attracted by the school's setting in this beautifully sylvan area. It reminded me so much of home - and how I missed home! That was over three years ago, and I was lucky to get the job.'

'Won't you ever go back to Cheptais, Mum? After all, Papa's house is officially yours now.'

'I would like to, but not until Matthew and Crispin are married. Nevertheless, when I give up teaching, I think I would really enjoy retiring there.'

The meal was over. They went back and sat round the low table and drank tea.

'Mum, do you know who this rich American is who has paid my fees?'

'The rich American who paid your fees? Who said it was a rich American?'

'The headmaster. He wasn't sure, but some Americans had visited the school and he thought one of them might have heard of my plight. You see the money was sent anonymously. No-one in the school knew who it was. It can't be anyone I know, can it?'

'Yes, it can. Who do you think it was?'

'I really haven't any idea.'

'Well, it was me.'

'You Mum? But Mum, why did you pay for my school fees when you couldn't be sure I was your son?'

'I took a chance. I thought if you were mine then all would be well. If you weren't, then I would at least have made sure my exceptionally gifted student was back in school. The school had your home address, so I knew the letter would come to you whoever you were. I couldn't ask for your address myself because it would've given the game away. Anyway, you don't have to worry about fees anymore. I can well afford to pay right up until the time you leave school.'

'Oh, I'm so grateful for that. And thanks too for the pocket money. You know the school meals are not that great and I used to be envious of those who supplemented their food by going to the tuck shop. Sometimes my friend Simeon would take pity on me and buy me a treat. He was so kind to me after that fight with Kamau. You heard about that I expect?'

'Yes, I did. I thought the headmaster handled the matter with great understanding.'

'You should have seen Grandfather's face when I read the letter to him saying my fees had been paid. He was jumping for joy and he hugged me so hard. He was terribly upset not being able to raise the fees. He believed he had let me down badly, and in a way, he felt he had let down you and Papa as well.'

'Poor old Elias, I can understand how he felt.'

'I wish he could see us together now.'

'I know what he would say.'

'What would he say?'

'It's divine providence!' and they both giggled.

For Winstone it was almost unbelievable to be able to share stories and laugh with his mother after such a long time apart and not knowing whether she was alive or not. This was the beginning of a new relationship. The last time they had been together he was a little child, totally dependent on her for his daily life. Now he was mature and talking to her almost as an equal. Now they thrilled at each other's company after such a long time apart. He wondered how different their relationship would have been if they had not been separated for such a long time. Would they still have felt as close to each other as they did now? What had caused him to fear just a few hours ago had turned into the most joyous event in his life, joy that that spread over him like a mantle, warm and glowing, an ecstasy which suffused heart and soul and mind.

It was then that Delia struck a more sombre note. 'But you know Wanyonyi, all this puts us in a very tricky situation. Nobody must know you are my son, neither in school nor at home. Imagine what would happen. People would wonder why your name was Wamalwa and mine was Okomo and why I never said that you were my son when you first came to school. They would wonder why you told people you were an orphan. They would wonder what you were trying to hide because nobody in their right mind is going to believe this remarkable coincidence that you and I found each other by accident. It would seem all too improbable. Because you are good at art and I give you a lot of attention they would say it was favouritism. They would wonder why I allowed you to be sent home for lack of fees. And word might get back to Cheptais that I was still alive and then they could hunt me down and I would have to face up to

Matthew or even Crispin. I would be unable to pretend to them that I was already married to a Mr. Okomo.

Then again, if you told them at home you had found your mother, other questions would be asked. If I can afford your fees now why didn't I pay them at the beginning? They would have said the *harambee* was raised under false pretences and that would not only embarrass your grandfather but make people turn away from him for being insincere. It wouldn't do my reputation any good either. You see, although we're both so happy to have found each other we're both going to have to be very disciplined to maintain that happiness and it isn't going to be easy. One slip of the tongue and the rat will be out of the bag. Then we'll both suffer.'

'You know Mum, I'm so overcome meeting you and being with you, the thought of the consequences hadn't entered my head.'

'I know, and I'm so sorry to have inflicted this on you. It makes me feel bad.'

'But Mum, you can't blame this on yourself. We would never have been in this predicament if Papa hadn't have died, and he couldn't help that. There's one thing though that bothers me. Absalom has stood by me and helped me through difficult times, and he's going to notice a difference in me when I go home. I'll not be able to pretend to him that I still have no mother. He'll see through that. He's very perceptive; sometimes I think he can read my thoughts. We've always been close and said we would hide nothing from each other. I think he's absolutely trustworthy. Do you think he's the one person I can tell that I have found you?'

'Well, Wanyonyi, you're fifteen now. I leave that decision to you. You're old enough to assess the situation yourself and make up your own mind. What we have to turn our attention to now is to decide how we handle each other in school. In class and indeed out of class, I shall have to treat you exactly as I've done in the past and that's going to be difficult for both of us. There's really no alternative if we're to keep up this pretence. It's tough I know, but there must be no hint of familiarity otherwise others will begin to suspect something: no smiling, no looking in each other's eyes, no favouritism, nothing like that. Instead, I suggest we make a point of spending every Sunday afternoon together here in my home. Then we can really be mother and son. You can stay for a meal in the evening and we can enjoy each other's company to our heart's content without others knowing our real relationship. It's sad we have to forfeit our openness for the sake of our happiness but that's how it's going to be for the next three years while you're at school. After that we'll no longer have to play this game.'

§

Winstone was with friends when he went into the dining hall for breakfast.

'Where were you yesterday evening, Wani?' asked Simeon. 'You didn't come in for your supper and you crept into bed late. At first I thought you'd been sent home again - until I saw your suitcase under your bed.'

'Mrs. Okomo left a note with the secretary saying she wanted to see me. She wanted to plan this term's work and she's suggested I come to her house for extra tuition on Sunday afternoons. It's a bit embarrassing really. I don't want it to be seen as favouritism.'

'I don't see why it should,' said Simeon. 'After all, Mr. Magondu takes us for extra football training on a regular basis doesn't he, Brian?' turning to another boy. 'Yeah, every Saturday morning. He regards us as having lots of potential and you know what competition is like between rival school teams. He wants us to come out on top.'

'And I get extra tuition in swimming,' said another boy. 'That's the advantage of having teachers living on the campus and why the school has such a good reputation for sport. I don't see why the same shouldn't apply to art, Wani. You're far better at painting and drawing than the rest of us.'

Winstone realised that this was the start of the pretence which was going to rule his life over the next three years.

CHAPTER SEVENTEEN

Coming home at the end of term, Winstone marvelled at the change of circumstances from when he had set out for school. Then he had been full of foreboding at the thought of meeting Mrs. Okomo, never really believing she could be his mother even though she had claimed to be. Apart from his father's death, all the shadows that had plagued him since childhood - the loss of his mother, his treatment at the hands of his uncles, the tyranny of Bruce, and the lack of school fees - had melted away. It was a joyous homecoming. The sun was shining out of a blameless blue sky. The light washed over his face and warmth suffused his body as if it was a blessing. It seemed to him all his woes were over. The past had been a test of his endurance and resilience and, hard though it had been, he could see that it was not without a purpose. He had grown the stronger and more mature for it, sure of himself and ready to face whatever the future would bring him.

'Well,' said Elias as he met Winstone walking towards the house, 'what was it like to be back at school?'

'Absolutely fabulous. I gained good results in all my exams, I'm in the archery team and we won against two other schools and now my voice has broken I'm singing in the senior choir.'

What a different homecoming from last time, Elias thought, both for his grandson and for himself. What a waste of talent it would have been but for that anonymous donor. As far as he knew, previous family members had never produced a youngster with such all-round ability. John had been bright and had obtained a well- paid job, but his academic ability could not match that of Winstone. It seemed to him such a shame his parents were not around to appreciate the accomplishments of the son they had brought into the world. That ability was innate. It hadn't been honed by family members wanting to see their offspring make good. Indeed, even if the parents had been alive, it was unlikely they would have had the capability to advance his education.

'What are you thinking, Grandfather?'

Elias stood silent, eying him. 'I was thinking, did you find out who that generous person was who paid your fees and has enabled my clever grandson to excel at school? Was it an American?'

'It certainly wasn't an American. That I'm sure of, but what I can say is that my fees are guaranteed for the rest of the time I'm at that school.'

'I'm so grateful for that whoever it is. A boy with your ability is rare in these parts. One such as you, needs all the support and encouragement he can get.'

When Absalom saw him, he said, 'You've grown! You're a cheat! We said we would share everything. You're much taller than me and your voice has deepened. You owe me a bit of your height and some of your voice!'

'Ha, ha, I can't do that, but I do have something else to share with you.'

'Is it a girl friend?'

'Not exactly. You don't find many girlfriends in a boy's school, but it does concern a woman and it's a secret we have to keep to ourselves. Let's go into the house and I'll tell you about it.'

'A woman?'

'Yes, a real live woman, don't you know!'

It gave Winstone a great sense of relief to tell Absalom about his mother. He had longed to express to someone the joy he felt at finding her. That joy had been pent up in him for a whole term. Joy was not something to keep to yourself. Joy had to be shared and shared joy was joy redoubled. That joy expressed, was not only intensified in Winstone, but it gladdened Absalom as well.

'I'm just so happy for you,' he said, 'and of course it'll be a deadly secret for both of us to keep. I've heard so much about your Mum I would really like to meet her.'

'You shall,' said Winstone, 'in the course of time. I promise.'

Winstone had not been back at school for long before he received a letter from Uncle John. He thought it strange, since nobody had written from home before. It seemed it must be important, and he hoped it did not contain bad news. It read as follows;

"Dear Winstone,

This letter will probably come as a surprise to you, and I can assure you is not bad news. My father is so impressed by your progress at school and in particular your examination results that he has asked to visit you. As you know he does not like travelling by car and has requested we travel by bus. We therefore plan to travel by local bus to Bungoma and thereafter to Nairobi. Grandfather has a cousin living in a village outside the city and we shall break our journey there overnight. We plan to be with you mid-morning on Saturday 20th of March. Please let me know by letter if this is

inconvenient. If I hear nothing from you, I will
assume this arrangement is acceptable.
  Yours, Uncle John."

The following Sunday Winstone showed the letter to his mother.

'Oh dear,' she exclaimed. 'I just hadn't expected this situation. This could be a real problem for us. I would never have guessed Elias would travel this far. Your uncle, yes, but not Elias. I don't think he has ever been much further than Bungoma. Nairobi is going to be so different for him. He'll find the place a shock. He'll have no concept of what a city is like. I don't know how well he will cope. At least he'll have John to guide him round. Nevertheless, I think it's remarkable he's so impressed with you that he wants to undertake what to him will seem like a pilgrimage. I think you should be really pleased with yourself. I'm just so thankful they have chosen to come on a Saturday when I shan't have to teach. This situation will have to be handled very carefully. I'll make a point of staying indoors all day to keep out of harm's way and when he and John arrive you'll have to be very careful indeed what you say to them. Obviously, there can be no mention of me.'

'It's going to be a day of deception, Mum. I hate the idea of it. I've always been honest and truthful. They know full well that I admire my art teacher. They're certainly going to ask to see the art room. What am I to say if they ask after you? I hope I can keep my nerve. I'll just have to say that since it's a Saturday there are no lessons and most teachers are away for the day. This is going to be a hard task for me.'

'I know it'll be an ordeal for you Wanyonyi. I'm sorry you have to go through with it. But it's for both our sakes. I'll be thinking of you and willing you on all the time. It'll be a test of your endurance. Tell your school mates you're going to be occupied all day. Then nobody will miss you and when the visit is over you must come and tell me how it went. I doubt they'll spend more than a couple of hours here. Your grandfather will find the visit tiring after the long journey on the Friday followed by his experience of Nairobi the next day.'

John had wisely not set an exact time to arrive at the school. Traffic in the city was so chaotic it was virtually impossible to determine when one might arrive. On the Saturday morning Winstone went down to the main gate and sat with the watchman until his uncle and grandfather appeared up the road. Winstone walked to meet them. Elias was already looking tired. John held his arm to help the old man along. They shook hands and Winstone led them into the school grounds. Grandfather seemed confused. The sheer brutality of the city with its high-rise buildings, the noise and bustle, the teeming traffic, the pollution and the hard pavements he had to walk along had unnerved him. As soon as they entered the grounds and he discovered the school was in a green haven he asked to sit down while he recovered. There were no seats, so they sat on the ground beneath the trees. After they had rested for a while they walked up to the school.

'My!' said Grandfather, looking at the main entrance with its flagpole, its tower and the surrounding two storey buildings, 'this is a huge place. How do you find your way around?'

'It takes only a day or two.' Winstone assured him. 'The prefects showed us round on our first day and we soon got the hang of it.'

Since it was Saturday most of the school was out on the playing fields and those living locally had gone home for the weekend. This meant they had the school largely to themselves. Grandfather was impressed by the quality of the classrooms with solid floors and glass in the windows but he was overcome when Winstone took him into the chapel.

'This is beyond belief,' he said, scratching his head and turning to his grandson. 'It's beautiful! Just look at all that carved wood and those huge windows. I've never seen the like of it. I don't think there can be a bigger church than this anywhere else in the world.'

'Oh yes there is,' said Winstone. 'We study architecture as well as art and we've read about cathedrals in England. Some of them are hundreds of years old and so huge they took two hundred years to build!' Then, pointing to the choir stalls, he said, 'Grandfather, this is where I stand when I sing in the choir. I used to be in the front row but now my voice has broken I stand behind with the senior choristers. It's a pity you're not here tomorrow, you would've enjoyed the singing. There are about twenty- five boys in the choir'

'Do you use a drum to keep time as we do at home?'

'Oh no,' said Winstone, 'we have a choir master to keep time and there's an organ that accompanies the singing.'

Grandfather was stunned when he saw the size of the organ. 'You mean this great machine can make a noise?'

'Yes. You see all these pipes; they all play different notes. The small ones make the high notes and these really big thick ones can make a thunderous sound.'

'I can't imagine what it must be like.'

'They have organs in the bigger churches in Nairobi. Our choir master took us to the Anglican cathedral once, so we could hear the quality of their singing. It was very impressive. Sometimes you can hear an organ being played on the radio on a Sunday. When you're at home you should listen out for it.'

Towards the end of their tour round the school they came to the art room. Delia knew they would have to pass by her bungalow and kept an eye open for them. Standing well back from the window she saw them walking towards her home. Elias was pointing and all three of them stopped outside the gate. Why had they stopped here of all places? Why hadn't Winstone made them walk past? Surely, he wasn't going to invite them in! Delia sank down on the floor out of sight, horrified they were going to come up the path. Had Winstone said something he shouldn't have done? No-one else at home would have known about her presence in the school except her son. She listened intently, not knowing what she would do if they called on her. The door was not locked. They could easily walk in. What would she do or say if they did? She crawled into the bedroom for safety. She felt a fool for not going away for the day, but she had been desperate to catch a glimpse of John and Elias whom she had not seen for twelve long years. These were her own close relatives who believed she was dead. How she would have loved to rush out to greet them and reassure them she was alive and well, and that she and her beloved son were reunited. She listened for what seemed an age but could have been only a matter of minutes. She didn't hear the gate open nor did she hear footsteps coming up to the door. Had they perhaps moved away? After a while she got up cautiously and peered out of the window. Nobody was around. They had passed on.

It was perhaps the art room which was to be the high point of the visit. Winstone knew they would be impressed. After all, the other classrooms had nothing to show for the work carried out in them. There might have been a few equations left on the blackboard in the maths room and there was a whole range of equipment on display in the science block but there was nothing to show for the work of individual students. The gym had nothing to offer except a few climbing ropes, some dumb-bells, weights and bars and a vaulting horse. In the language room Elias had opened a textbook and asked what language it was.

'French,' Winstone replied.

'Well, who speaks that language?' Elias asked.

'The French mainly, but French is also spoken in Canada and a number of African countries as well.'

'You don't speak French do you, so why learn it? You learnt English at primary school, and I thought that was unnecessary.'

'I may need French one day. Besides, I had to learn English. In this school everyone speaks English and all textbooks and lessons are in English. It's the same in every secondary school, and you would have had to learn English too when you were young if you had remained at school long enough to finish your studies.'

'But that's being disloyal to our country. We're Kenyans and everybody can manage perfectly well with Swahili.'

'Dad,' interjected John, 'English is one of the most used languages in the world. I had to learn it at school. The few Swahili speaking countries in Africa have populations too small to print secondary school textbooks in that language. It's just not cost effective, if you know what I mean. Besides if we want to communicate with other countries around the world English is the best language to learn because it's a language so many people use.'

'So much for your education then,' said Elias grumpily. 'Nobody here will understand me if I speak to them. What good is that?'

'If you speak in Swahili they will, but not if you speak in our native tongue.'

In a way Elias was envious of his grandson who at his young age was far better informed than he was, and grumpy too at having his own education cut short through the lack of school fees. He cheered up however when he entered the art room. Unlike the other classrooms it was colourful and full of interest. The walls were covered with the work of students. There was all manner of artwork: paintings, drawings, designs and models. Two students had come in during their free time to complete some of their assignments. Winstone introduced them to his grandfather and uncle.

Elias peered over the shoulder of one of them. 'My!' he said in Swahili, 'that's a fine drawing.'

'Thank you sir,' the boy answered, 'but Wani is by far the best artist around here. He outshines us all. Just look at that picture over there, sir.'

Winstone was embarrassed. 'Wani is my nick-name in school he explained.'

John and Elias moved over to where the picture hung. It was framed and in oils and larger than the others on the wall.

'You painted that?' asked John. Winstone nodded. He knew he had been blessed with an exceptional ability but was modest with it.

'I know where that is!' exclaimed Elias in delight. 'It's Mount Elgon from Sirisia!'

'Yes', said Winstone. 'You know, when I was sent home from school Grandfather, I asked whether you could give me some bus money. I caught some early transport, got out at Sirisia, sat by the roadside and sketched this scene. It's one of my favourites. I was using the largest of the canvasses you gave me, Uncle John. Several people passed and stopped to see what I was doing. I wasn't used to people watching me sketch. I don't think any of them had seen an artist at work before. I found it rather embarrassing. Then a girl came along on her way to school and she wouldn't go away. She must have stood by me for an hour or so watching how I put the picture together. She said she wished she could draw like me. I told her she would be late for school. She said she would rather be late and punished than not see me finish the sketch. I was going to work on it at home to turn the sketch into a painting, but when I learnt I was going back to school I decided to wait until I had all the facilities and the advice of my teacher here. Working in oils is not easy.'

'My!' said Elias again in admiration, 'this really is lovely. You can see it's early morning from the shadows on the fields and the smoke curling up from newly lit fires in those little homes and that fresh blue sky and wisps of clouds above. How I wish Martha could see it.'

John too, was impressed and said how glad he was that he and his sister and brothers had given him the canvasses. Elias moved along the wall to another picture, also in oils.

'Oh, I like this one,' he said. 'This too is beautiful! A lot of skill has gone into this one too.'

'Yes, my mother...' Shocked at what he had started to say, Winstone stopped in mid-sentence. He had made the ultimate blunder. Furious with himself, he had somehow to save the situation. He began again. 'My mother would have liked that one I am sure, if she had been here... I... I mean, alive.'

'I'm sure she would, don't you think John?'

'Yes, she would, Dad. She had real artistic talent. It's a pity she's not here with us. She would've loved to see what her son can achieve. She must've passed on her artistic ability to you Winstone. Who painted this one, do you know? Not you I suppose?'

'No. I didn't paint it.' He began to panic. 'Actually, I'm not sure who did.'

'Oh, come on Wani,' said one of the boys listening to the conversation, 'Our teacher Mrs. Okomo painted that one, don't you remember?'

'Oh yes, now I remember, it was Mrs. Okomo,' he said weakly. 'Yes, I had forgotten that.'

'As well as being a good teacher, she is a fabulous artist herself,' the boy continued, addressing Elias and John. 'She's such a kind person and devotes a lot of time to those of us who have talent. She says paintings are a way of expressing our feelings, not only our feelings but arousing the feelings of those who enjoy looking at them. You see, sir, the sentiments the artists have expressed in those two pictures you have just been looking at have been passed onto you and given you enjoyment, isn't that so, sir?

'Thank-you. Yes, you're right,' said Elias. 'You said that eloquently. It's a great observation and I admire you for it. There are times when I've chided my grandson for spending so much of his time painting and drawing. I'd not looked at it that way. Out in the country people can't afford to buy pictures so we have no experience of appreciating them.'

'I should really like to meet your teacher to congratulate her on the way her pupils look up to her,' John said.

'I... I don't think she's available today,' ventured Winstone. 'I think she's gone out somewhere.'

He could have wept. The strain on him was almost beyond endurance. How was it they had been struck by his mother's painting, virtually mourning her death and wishing she was still alive when in fact she was alive and well and living not more than a couple of hundred yards away! How she would have loved to show them her picture herself. How she would have loved to have shown off her son's artistic ability. There was she, longing to declare herself to them, and they, wishing she could have been here with them. It was not a physical barrier that kept them apart, but an illusive mental barrier. It was none other than Winstone himself who was maintaining that mental barrier and that barrier induced by his conscience was driving him virtually to distraction. The worst of it was: he knew both sides of the situation. But for that conceived barrier he had the means of bringing them together within a matter of minutes. It was a huge temptation he wrestled with. What a joyful occasion that meeting would be, but what unacceptable circumstances would follow!

Elias was tired. The experience of the bustling city and the tour round the school had been exhausting for him and he was indicating to John it was time to leave. For Winstone this came as a relief from the pretence he was having to maintain. The tour over, they walked back to the main building. Elias was looking anxiously around the grounds.

'What's the matter, Father?' John asked.

'I need to urinate. Find me a spot somewhere.'

'You can't urinate in the grounds, Dad. That's forbidden. Winstone will show you where the toilets are. They're inside the buildings somewhere.'

'Urinate inside the buildings? That's unhealthy!'

'No, it's not Dad. It's common practice.'

Unwillingly Elias was led to the toilet block.

'There,' said Winstone, 'you pee here,' pointing to the urinal.

'What! pee on that wall! That's disgraceful! That's what dogs do.'

'That's what humans do as well, Dad, but you don't have to cock your leg like a dog,' said John with a grin.

Elias didn't think that remark was funny 'But where do I stand? Why is this wall so long?'

'Because when there are a lot of us peeing; we need the room,' Winstone said.

'What! You mean several of you stand here at the same time. Isn't there any modesty in this place?'

'When you've finished you can wash your hands here. You turn on the tap like this and you get hot water and you turn on the other tap to get cold water. Turn them off afterwards and wipe your hands on the paper towel that comes out of this dispenser,' said John. 'Just pull the paper then a piece will come out. When you've wiped your hands place it in the basket below.' Then he and Winstone walked away to give the old man some privacy.

When he came out Elias was full of questions. 'Where does the water come from? What happens if you want to do more than pee? Where do they keep the bowls for having a bath?'

They went back inside. Winstone explained water was pumped out of the ground and stored in a high tank so that the water ran out of taps by gravity. He showed Elias a toilet and explained you don't put your feet on the seat and squat as if you're using a long drop latrine, but instead you sit and do your business, and since no leaves grow in buildings you use toilet paper instead to wipe yourself. Then he demonstrated the showers. Elias said it was just like standing in the rain.

'Yes', said Winstone, 'but rain is always cold. With these showers you can choose to have hot or cold or warm rain.'

When they were ready to leave Elias thanked Winstone and said, apart from his artwork, he thought the most marvellous thing about the school was the toilet block.

'My boy,' he said as he was departing, 'I'm immensely proud of you. I couldn't have wished for a better grandson. May God bless you and be with you always.'

CHAPTER EIGHTEEN

That evening Winstone arrived at his mother's home to update her on the day's experiences. Recounting the episode in the art room he said in a way he wished he had been dead. It was the most agonising occasion he could remember.

'There was you here and they there only a short distance away. They were commiserating over your demise, you not being able to see your son's painting nor that of Mrs. Okomo and... and wanting to meet up with my art teacher whom I had to say was not around. Uncle John said he wanted to congratulate you on the way you inspire your pupils. It would've been a farce if it hadn't been so sad. I wanted to cry but I managed not to.'

'I'm sure they admired your picture, Wanyonyi. It really is a lovely painting, the best you've done so far. That must've been some comfort.'

'I suppose it was, although it didn't make much impact at the time. They were very taken with your painting though. I made a terrible mistake and started to say you were the artist and then had to change it quickly to say if you would have been alive you would have liked it. I don't think they noticed anything strange about what I said, but what I had to say was very painful to me. How I hated that pretence. The situation was so unreal. I was desperate to say you've got it all wrong; my mother isn't dead; she's wonderfully and beautifully alive; come and meet her, meet the creator of that painting; she's living only a few yards away; she's longing to see you, just as much as you're longing to see her; come and give my beloved mother a hug and rejoice in her company.'

'I can understand how you felt. I would've loved to invite them into my house, sat them down, given them tea and talked about the old times.'

Delia was wiping a tear from her eyes. 'I had a nasty experience too. I knew you would have to pass here to get to the art room and I was desperate to see your grandfather and John after all these years, so I kept a look out for you as far away from the window as I could get, yet still being able to see them. But you didn't walk past. You stopped in front of the gate. I was frightened you'd said something, and they were going to come in. I sank down on the floor out of sight, crawled into the bedroom as a precaution, and waited and waited. But nothing happened, and you must have gone on.'

'It was very embarrassing. Grandfather was taken by the neatness of the garden and wanted to know who lived here. I just said it was one of the teachers.'

'Well, I suppose it is a neat garden. I employ one of the fourth-form boys to cut the hedges and grass. He's glad to have some pocket money.'

'That would've been Martin Munyalo, wouldn't it? He got talking to Grandfather, said what a good teacher you were. Pointed out to him the psychological value of painting. I think Grandfather was impressed, said he had put the case for painting eloquently, even confessed he had chided me for spending so much time on my painting and drawing when I lived at home!'

'Well that was something then! All the same I know he loved to look at my paintings and drawings. Munyalo also comes from a poor background. His home is in a remote village on the edge of Akamba territory. I remember him telling me the same story I've heard from elsewhere. At his primary school no-one could afford pencils and paper and when he first went there and was being taught the alphabet, he had to practice writing the letters with his fingers on the dirt floor he was sitting on. It makes you realise what a stark contrast there is in this country of ours. There was he in his village writing with his fingers on the ground while here in Nairobi we have embraced the computer age.

You were saying about Grandfather chiding you for your drawings. Do you know whether any of my drawings have been saved?'

'They're all in that drawer as you left them. You know Mum, it was your art- work that inspired me. I would copy those drawings time and time again until I got them perfect. It kept me occupied all the time I was alone in the house. You see, I had to keep away from those twins as much as I could. Aunt Catherine was always so supportive. Once, on my birthday, she brought me a pencil sharpener, a pad of paper and an ink well in which I could put water without spilling over my paintings. It was all wrapped up in beautiful paper. Grandmother made me open the parcel carefully, so I didn't tear it. I kept it and put it away in the drawer you kept your drawings in, thinking I might need to use it for a special parcel one day. And I did need it. It was the paper I wrapped your scarf in!'

'How wonderful, Wanyonyi! How very wonderful! What a wonderful thing to happen. You must have had a premonition at the time.'

'I think I did. I never really believed you had died despite what my grandparents said. But at the same time, as I said, it caused me a lot of worry because I thought you might have remarried and had children I didn't know about and whom I would perhaps never meet. You know that boy Kamau? he called you a whore. Said you had left me to chase after other men. That's why I fought him. I was raging! I was going to protect your name whatever it cost.'

'That was noble of you, Wanyonyi, thank you. I wondered why you two had got into a fight. Now I know. I don't like the thought of people fighting, but in this case, I'm proud of you and I think Papa would've been proud of you too.'

That evening in bed in the dormitory Winstone mused over the events of the day. It seemed obvious to him both grandfather and John were convinced his mother had died while he, of course, was aware beyond all doubt she was alive. It seemed it was all a matter of perception. The thought occurred to him that our senses inform our thoughts and our thoughts direct our perception of life. Sometimes our senses play tricks on us and corrupt our thoughts and subsequently our perception. There was a railway line near his school. If you looked along the track, your eyes told you in the distance the rails came together, but in reality, they didn't. They remained the same distance apart, but unless you knew better you would believe they did come together. It was a bit like that with his grandparents. Because his mother had been missing for such a long time, their memory of her had faded and they sensed she was dead. It became a feature of their thoughts. They had said she was dead so many times, the thoughts became their perception and they really came to believe she was dead. If they had rejected their senses and the thoughts arising from them, their perception might have been different. He remembered a saying he had once heard: "Two prisoners behind bars. One looked down and saw mud through the bars, the other looked up and saw heaven full of stars." Both were in the same predicament, but their perceptions were different. One depressed, the other inspired. It seemed to him life experiences had no fixed boundaries and life was an illusion depending upon how you perceived it. Absalom as a young child was a weakling. His senses told him so, yet he overruled the attendant thoughts and by changing his perception of himself became an excellent sportsman.

Winstone thought back to the night following the drawing he made of his uncle's lorry. He'd had a dream. He was painting a picture of all the things dear to him. It was full of flowers and trees and mountains set under a brilliant blue sky. Suddenly Papa was standing beside him. There he was with his cheery smile, his bushy eyebrows and twinkling eyes. He was looking at the picture being painted. Then he turned to Winstone and said, "One day my son, you will become a famous artist." At that moment he had woken up. Dreams fade but this one was even now fresh in his mind as if it had been only yesterday. It was one of life's illusions. He knew Papa was dead – his senses told him so – yet through that dream which seemed so real, he was convinced his father was still alive even though out of sight and on another plane of existence. It seemed to him that even death was an illusion. After all, didn't Jesus prove that?

Still musing, the thought came to him that our world was one of opposites – hot and cold, up and down, good and evil – and it was through those opposites we experienced life. Yet even these were illusions. If a rocket took off from Cape Canaveral it would seem to be going up, but if it took off from somewhere on the other side of the world it would still seem to be going up. So where was up and where was down? Those opposites were illusions just like the rail track. Religion maintained God was the "all of everything." If that was true, then, being the all of everything, God could know no opposites. God might know it was God, but it couldn't experience being God. So maybe God had created the world of opposites as a means of experiencing itself. Maybe God was doing its experiencing through ourselves. Maybe that was the purpose of our lives! Maybe the misconception John and his grandfather had about his mother and the concept he had of her was for the moment God's little joke. After all, if God was doing its experiencing through ourselves, He would know all about jokes.

'I've been thinking how you could hone your ability to paint portraits,' Delia said to Winstone when they next met. 'It's all very well having classmates sitting as models for quick sketches, but I want you and one or two others in the class to concentrate on more formal portraits. That would probably have to be done out of class. It would mean finding someone to sit for you for long periods at a time and I think they should have some financial inducement for doing so. There's enough money in my art fund to cover that. As far as you're concerned, is there anyone you can think of who might make a suitable model?'

'Presumably we could use the art room out of class time?'

'Yes, you would have to do that.'

Winstone considered for a moment. 'There's only one person I can think of and that is Lepish Sipaya. He always travels between home and school wearing his *nanga* and he carries his school uniform with his other belongings. I've seen him stride into school in that long red garment and his sandals and he looks magnificent. I would love to paint a portrait of him, but I don't know whether he would allow me to. He never has pocket money, so he might be tempted to sit for me if he was to earn something. The trouble is he doesn't bring his beads and earrings with him. I could make the initial sketches of him this term if he was willing and then he might be persuaded to bring his warrior beads and ornaments with him next term.'

'I've seen him only in passing. I don't know him really because, as you know, he opted out of art lessons. He certainly has a presence and a face full of character. It seems to me, Wanyonyi, he would be a good subject, especially if you can capture his facial expression. How does he spend his spare time?'

'He plays a lot of cricket and occasionally football and he's excellent at archery. I wish I could do as well as he does. His accuracy is amazing. I suppose it comes from throwing spears. He told me they practice spear throwing from childhood.'

'See what he says. If he agrees, I'd like to talk to the two of you together so that we can arrange the setting of the portrait. I think the best medium might be acrylic paint. The colours are bright and easier to work with than oils.'

For Lepish, sitting for a portrait was a novel idea and he liked the thought of earning some pocket money. It was agreed he would bring his warrior ornaments with him, but he didn't think the police would allow him to come with his spear or shield. A week or two later the sketching began, and it provided Winstone with an opportunity to find out what life as a Maasai was like. Talking while Winstone was making the initial sketches was a good idea since it encouraged Lepish to relax and in turn enable Winstone to make a more authentic portrait.

'Why do you live the way you do instead of the way we live?' asked Winstone. 'Why do you walk when you could ride in a vehicle? Why are you content to live in stick and mud huts? Why do you wear basic clothing when you could wear shirts and trousers like us?'

Lepish did not answer immediately. He sat on his chair playing with the small club he carried with him while he gathered his thoughts together. Then he turned and faced Winstone.

'That's a lot of questions you're asking. I'll try to explain. First of all, we walk because it's our custom. The land is dear to us and we don't like to be separated from it in vehicles if we can avoid them. You see, babies are born on the ground. When we die, we're laid out on the ground. The ground gives us grass for our cattle to eat. From our cattle we get blood and milk which is our basic food and gives us life. We also get skins from them to make our huts waterproof. The ground also gives us trees and we make a framework for our huts from their branches. It's that wood together with the iron the ground yields from which we make our bows and arrows and swords and spears. Even the red ochre with which we colour ourselves comes from the ground. You see, we revere the land. Nobody can claim to own any of it. It's our duty to preserve it for future generations.

You asked, why do we live the way we do. You see, we don't look at the world in the same way as you do. Our values are the opposite of yours. When you judge a person be it man or woman, you ask yourself, "What have they achieved? How much land or property do they own? What position of importance do they occupy? How wealthy are they? What kind of car do they drive? What is the quality of the clothes they wear?" You adulate your footballers and pay them vast sums of money because of their performance on the field. You treat your film stars and your television personalities in the same way. You don't take into account the quality and character of the person. Your attitude reflects your overriding concern with performance and materialism. We look at a person quite differently. When we judge a person we say, "How brave are they? How much respect do they command? How honest and trustworthy are they? How reliable are they? How much wisdom do they have?" We see the person for what they are. It is the quality of each individual which reflects the quality of the society in which they live. So many of your rich people are made corrupt by the amount of money they earn while others starve for want of food. Being rich doesn't necessarily make people happy and in any case it's pointless. You can't take your riches with you when you die. What does that say for the quality of your way of living? There's no equality, no sharing.'

Winstone put his pencil down for a minute while he considered what Lepish had said. 'Gosh, I never thought of life like that.'

'Then the cornerstone of our society,' Lepish continued, 'is "*nkanyit*" which is the word we use for universal respect. Every person from the youngest babe to the oldest person is entitled to respect. Every human being is a child of *Ngai*, or what you call God, and just as we respect God, so we respect each individual. It is a sin in our eyes if due respect is not accorded to every person. Respect in our terms means not only being polite but sharing what one has and caring for everyone's needs. I don't seem to see that in your kind of society. Look at the children sleeping out on the streets at night because they have nowhere else to go. Where is your respect for them? Where is your care for them? What about those people on the point of starvation all over the world? Where is your respect for them, or for those desperately ill who can't afford to go to a doctor or a hospital while others are so rich, they can afford private medical treatment? You see, as I explained to our headmaster, without respect society breaks down.'

'When did you say that to the headmaster?'

'When I went to see him after your fight with Bruce.'

'You went to see the headmaster?'

'Yes, I was sickened by Bruce's lack of respect for everyone except himself. I felt I had a duty to try to stop it. I explained that Bruce's lack of respect was equally as painful and damaging to others as were the punches you gave him and that one of you shouldn't be expelled without the other.'

'So that is why he told us we had to learn to respect each other and why neither of us were expelled! Lepish, I really appreciate what you did for us that day and why the bullying stopped once and for all. And you kept quiet about it. I admire you for your modesty. You know, you make me wish I could experience what it is like to live with your people. I think I would certainly admire them.'

'I could arrange for that if you really feel you could spend a few days living our way. It might be hard for you, but you could do some sketches too if you wanted to. We don't like people taking photographs of us because some believe they can take away our souls, but you would be welcome to do sketches. That would be great because seeing sketches might introduce people to the way we live. Very few people have ever seen or understood our culture.'

'So then, tell me why you've decided to come into the city to go to school and live as we do?'

'That's because I'm passionate about the way we live and our values. I would wish to see a fairer, more compassionate, more understanding world. My greatest wish is to become a teacher myself and to share our values with your children, since children are so much more receptive to new ideas than the majority of adults.'

§

When Winstone arrived home in the Easter holidays he was greeted by Crispin who had a broad smile on his face.

'I've got some news for you. I've become engaged to a girl from the next village. She's called Rose. She's very pretty. I think you will like her. Crispin took Winstone to meet her. She was a comely looking girl, a little younger than her husband-to-be, well built but not plump, with a generous smile and rather shy. Winstone thought she would make an excellent wife for Crispin and was very pleased for him.

'We plan to get married during your next school holiday. Mathew will be my best man. If you and Absalom would agree, I would like you to be ushers,' said Crispin. 'Absalom's sister Ellen, along with Petra will be bridesmaids.'

There had not been a wedding in the family in Winstone's lifetime although he had attended others in the community and had a good idea of what was entailed. He was glad Crispin was no longer to live as a lonely bachelor. Elias too, was pleased for Crispin and since he and Martha still suffered the loss of Delia, they welcomed the prospect of another woman joining the family.

'Well,' said Absalom, after Winstone had met Rose. 'What do you think of her?'

'I think she will make Crispin an excellent wife.'

'So do I. So that's one down and three to go.'

'What do you mean?'

'Matthew is likely to be the next to marry. He already has a girlfriend. Then it will be you and me.'

'But I don't have a girl-friend.'

'Nor have I but I'm always on the look-out!'

It was inevitable that Matthew was to be the next to marry and this time Winstone was to be best man. The wedding took place in November at the end of his third school year. By now he was a mature seventeen-year-old and a prefect at school. He had spent part of his school holidays living with Lepish's family and had made many sketches portraying the Maasai and their customs. Life on the plains had been an entirely new experience for him. Of course, he wasn't accustomed to living on a largely liquid diet of blood and milk so the family cooked rice for him. The smoke from the fire in the hut made his eyes sore and he had to get used to their negligible toilet facilities, yet he was surprised how easily he had accepted their way of living. He loved the camaraderie of the warriors. In their care, he roamed the land they shared with the lions, the elephants, the cheetahs and a panoply of other wild animals, without fear of them. Their closeness to nature and the freedom of the wide-open plains enthralled him. One day, he said to himself, 'I must introduce Absalom to this marvellous experience. It's something we should share together.'

Returning home during this, the long school holiday, he was intrigued to see how much Crispin and Matthew had developed the farm over the past year. It was no longer the smallholding he once knew. More land had been acquired and in addition to basic crops they had now branched out into the cultivation of specialist fruit and vegetables. These were sold in Bungoma and Eldoret markets, earning them more income than could be gained from local markets. They had employed extra hands from the village to help on the land and Absalom was in line to join the enterprise the following year after finishing his education.

'It's all thanks to you, Winstone,' he said. 'They want me to take a driving test when I leave school. Crispin needs to spend more time on the farm than he does at present. He wants me to take over the distribution side and reckons he can afford to buy a newer van when I start work, and I shall be responsible for driving it. I never imagined in my wildest dreams I would land a job like this. If you hadn't suggested I come to live with you and work on the farm, this opportunity would not have come my way.'

'Grandfather didn't talk much about the enterprise when I arrived home. He seemed resigned to leaving it in Crispin and Matthew's capable hands.'

'He's getting pretty old now and like most old people he doesn't accept new innovations very well. He doesn't mind me becoming an employee because he knows me but he's unhappy having other villagers working on his land. In a way he feels he is losing the ownership of it. Neither does he like the idea of his produce being sold to "foreign" markets and bought by people he doesn't know. He's opposed to the farm owning a new vehicle and the thought of me driving it. He says it's wrong I should risk my life on the roads at such a young age! I don't think he realises our standard of living is going to improve and that he and your grandmother will be able to live the rest of their days in relative comfort. My mum is much more forward looking. She's really pleased I'll have a future in the village rather than leaving to find employment elsewhere. Anyway, that's enough of that. What are your plans when you leave school Winstone?'

'I would like to carry on painting and find a market for my pictures, but Mum insists I go to university first. She says there's no guarantee that I'll make a worthwhile living as an artist. Much of the living would depend upon visitors to our country wanting to buy authentic pictures to take home with them. If I have a degree, there would be other options available to me. I could become a teacher or a lecturer in art for instance. I suppose she's right.'

'Well, I hope you become a really successful artist. Then you could rebuild this house of yours, add a studio and work from home. Perhaps it's selfish of me to say so, but I would miss you if you lived away permanently.'

'Actually, I would miss you too Absalom. In any case I could never live in a city. All my interests are in the countryside and it's rural life that inspires my art.'

CHAPTER NINETEEN

Winstone's last year at school was his best. He was well respected by everybody. He was mature, articulate and self-confident. To his surprise he was made head boy. Delia was proud of her son, especially as she had taken no part in his selection. She recognised that the hardships he had been through had played a significant part in forming his character. She often wished Jeremiah had lived long enough to see his son develop to maturity. He had always believed that Winstone had great potential though he would probably never have imagined he would become head boy of a prestigious national school in the capital as well as being an accomplished painter.

Delia was determined Winstone's ability should come to public notice and when she and Winstone met up at the beginning of term, she explained she had been in touch with somebody she knew who owned an art gallery in Nairobi and had taken along some of his work for him to see. Realising the dearth of paintings representing tribal life, the gallery owner was particularly interested in Winstone's sketches as well as his more formal work and offered to put on an exhibition in his gallery. A date was pencilled in which coincided with the end of the school year. Many of his clients were well off and he said November and December were particularly good sales months because of their closeness to the Christmas season. Looking at the quality of Winstone's paintings he had no doubt they would sell well.

'I suggest you spend your last year of art lessons working up those sketches into full blown paintings,' Delia advised Winstone. 'I'll oversee your work and make suggestions as necessary. Mr. Kagwe, the gallery owner has also agreed to exhibit one or two of my paintings as well. Then it will be a mother-and-son exhibition, but of course the emphasis will be on your work.'

'But Mum, are you sure that's wise? If you do that, our relationship will be revealed, and everybody will know I'm your son!'

'I don't see that as a problem Winstone. You'll have left school by then and with Crispin and Matthew both happily married, it won't matter if the truth comes out. In fact, it'll be a great relief to me when it does, as well as for you. You and I can then resume our proper relationship in public.'

His mother's confidence in the future was encouraging for Winstone. He was tired of deception. It sapped his self-esteem, lowered his morale, made him feel dishonest and a fake. It tarnished the joy he felt in being reconciled with his mother. Outwardly he was obliged to exemplify normality, inwardly he was burdened with perfidy. Now, knowing the end of deception was in sight, the spirit of liberation burned within him. Everything he turned to was accomplished with greater motivation whether it was his duties as head boy, his class work, his archery or his painting, and especially his painting. By the end of the school year there were some thirty portraits, landscapes, and scenes from tribal life framed and ready for exhibition. The cost of framing Winstone's output was considerable but Delia generously footed the bill.

After he had left school, his paintings and those few of Delia's were taken to the gallery to be arranged by Mr. Kagwe. There was to be a preview of the exhibition for invited guests, most of whom were invited by Mr. Kagwe, but included at Winstone's request were Absalom and Lepish. Winstone and Delia visited the gallery a couple of days before the preview. Winstone was filled with pride when he saw his work displayed but, as ever, modesty prevented him from showing it. He was however, shocked when he saw the price tags that had been attached to his work.

'Mum,' he said in a whisper, 'these prices are ridiculous. They'll never sell at those figures.'

Mr. Kagwe overheard him.

'My young man,' he said, coming across to him in the rather formal manner of an elder statesman, 'I've run this gallery for some twenty or so years. You can't tell me my business. I know my clients intimately. I know their tastes and I know what they're prepared to pay for a good picture. Let me be the judge of those prices.'

Winstone felt reprimanded. He painted and sketched for the sheer joy of it, not for any monetary reward. It was something he loved to do. It was an expression of his love of people and of nature. Although he was resolved to paint for a living, the cash value of his work had never entered his head. Mr. Kagwe might have liked his pictures and maybe even admired his skill as a painter, but in the end, it was, for him, a business, and he was out to make as much money as he could from the commission. The thought of his exhibition as a commercial exercise, like selling produce from a stall in the market, came as a shock.

'Mum,' he said, when they had left the gallery, 'how do you feel about your friend Mr. Kagwe seeing his gallery as a commercial enterprise rather than a platform for the expression of art?'

'My impression is that he does value pictures as an expression of art. He's bought many pictures for himself over the years. Indeed, he wouldn't be in this business if he didn't appreciate art. But if you want to be a painter you have to make a living, just as he does, and he's the go-between linking your work with those who'll buy your output. They buy pictures because it gives them pleasure, and a painting or indeed any other form of artistry is a lasting pleasure, not a fleeting one, and it'll be one his clients like enough to be prepared to pay good money for them.'

For Absalom, an invitation to go to Nairobi, let alone attend the preview with the great and good, was a challenge. He was nervous from the start. He was, he thought, basically an impoverished country boy from a humble background. He hadn't the graces and airs of a cultured individual. He was worried he wouldn't have the standard of bearing expected by the kind of city dwellers likely to attend such an event. He had bought a pair of reasonably good black shoes at the market and had saved enough money to purchase a suit when he arrived in the city, for there was no outlet for such clothes where he lived. Winstone had assured him by letter that he shouldn't be worried by such matters and had forwarded him his bus fare. Even the bus journey would be an ordeal. He had been to Bungoma several times but that was the furthest distance he had travelled from home. Now he would have to find his way to the Nairobi bus in Bungoma on his own and travel what seemed to him an immense distance to an environment he had heard much about from Winstone but could not imagine himself.

As previously arranged, Delia and Winstone met Absalom at the bus station in Nairobi. His journey had been uneventful, but like all newcomers to the city from rural Kenya he was completely overwhelmed by the noisy, aggressive, overpopulated capital.

'You're the so-called twin brother then,' Delia said, shaking hands and laughing. Delia's warm greeting put Absalom immediately at ease. 'I've heard so much about you from Winstone. We've met before you know, but you were only a baby then in your mother's arms.'

'I'm so glad you're here to greet me,' replied Absalom. 'I would've been petrified if I'd arrived here on my own. I've heard so many good things about you from Winstone that I've longed to meet you. I've promised I won't tell anyone we've met. I hope you can trust me. Winstone's grandparents thought I would be meeting just Winstone. I'm very glad you're with us because I've never shopped for clothes and I wouldn't know how to go about buying a suit.'

'We'll see to all that. In fact, I want to take you to the shops now before they close.'

At a gentleman's outfitters Absalom was handed a grey suit and a white shirt to try on. He looked embarrassed.

'Do I have to try it on here?' he asked.

Delia laughed. 'No, no, there's a fitting cubicle over there. Just go in and draw the curtain across and change in privacy.'

Even so, Absalom didn't feel comfortable taking his trousers off in a shop full of people. Somebody could easily draw the curtains aside and expose him to all and sundry. He changed as quickly as he could, his fingers stumbling over the buttons and buttonholes on the shirt. When he put the trousers on, he searched for the buttons to do up his flies. There were none. Surely men didn't go around with their flies undone. He fumbled around for a bit, nervous that he would have to go out into the shop again with his flies open. Then he found a little metal tag. He pulled it outwards, but it wouldn't come away. He fiddled with it and suddenly it started to move upwards and brought the two sides of material together. It was his first experience of a zip.

'You took a long time,' said Winstone as his friend reappeared.

'I found those buttons on my shirt fiddly and it took me ages to find how to close up my private parts.'

Delia and Winstone both laughed. 'I forgot. You won't have seen a zip before. It's the first of many smart things you're going to experience while you're here,' said Delia. 'Look, I've bought you a tie. You'll need to wear it with your shirt. And here are some socks for you.'

That evening Lepish met up with them at Delia's home in the school grounds. This time he wore a jacket, and trousers bought for when he was to start at university. It meant that on this occasion he had had to use public transport to reach Nairobi rather than walk and sleep under bushes as was his custom. He was very surprised to discover Mrs. Okomo was in fact Winstone's mother.

Turning to Winstone he said, 'Why didn't you tell me this before? You never told me anything about your mother. I thought she lived at your home in Cheptais.'

'It's a tribal matter,' explained Winstone. 'We live very different lives and our traditions are quite unlike yours.' He explained the circumstances that led to him and his mother being separated and then coming together again at school as the result of a coincidence.

For Delia it was a joy to entertain Winstone's closest friends.

'Do I have to keep your secret?' Lepish had asked, but Delia assured him that since Winstone had left school there was no longer any need so long as word didn't get back to the family in Cheptais. Delia had prepared a meal for all of them and after they had eaten, they fell to talking until late in the evening.

The preview at Mr. Kagwe's gallery was timed for six o'clock the following evening. The four of them left the school by taxi. Absalom relished wearing his new suit.

'It's a perfect fit,' he declared, 'and with my tie and shirt and new socks I feel like a man of the world and worth a million dollars!'

'You wear that at home at your peril. All the girls from miles around will be queuing up to marry you,' quipped Winstone. 'And they won't want you, sonny boy, it's your money they'll be after!'

They arrived at the gallery early. Mr. Kagwe greeted them on arrival and was introduced to Absalom and Lepish.

'It's the first time I've had the honour of welcoming a Maasai to my gallery, and especially one who has his own portrait hanging here. It's also a pleasure to have an exhibition devoted to the works of mother and son. All the paintings are priced,' he explained to Absalom and Lepish, 'and all those sold will be marked with a red dot. Have a good look round while you can. Once people arrive it'll get very crowded.'

As they walked around Absalom said, 'I see the one of Mount Elgon from Sirisia which I like so much has been sold already.'

'And so has Winstone's portrait of me,' added Lepish. 'I wonder who would have bought it?'

'Actually, neither have been sold and nor will they be,' said Winstone. 'They are reserved as a gift to each of you, yours for being such a good companion all these years Absalom, and yours Lepish for enabling me to do all those sketches of your people. And you know, Absalom, we agreed to share everything between us. It may be selfish of me to say so but I'm very fond of that painting of Mount Elgon and I wouldn't want anybody else to buy it. When you're married and hang it in your home, it will please me to come around to sneak a look at it from time to time!'

The gallery soon became crowded. Wine, soft drinks and nibbles were served. There was much interest in Winstone's ethnic paintings as well as his landscapes. Mr.Kagwe's clients seemed to appreciate particularly the serious studies of Kenyan culture and countryside rather than the kitschy renderings sold in shops with tourists in mind. People were surprised a Maasai was among the invitees. Lepish was asked to explain the background to many of the paintings Winstone had made of his people. There was also a man with a camera who asked to take a photograph of Lepish next to his portrait. He also took a photograph of Winstone standing by the painting of Mount Elgon.

Winstone's headmaster was among the crowd and congratulated his former student handsomely. Later he cornered Delia.

'Your pupil has turned out some impressive work. I particularly liked the portrait of Lenana, the Maasai paramount chief. He tells me Sipaya asked him if he would make that portrait from a picture of him since he was such a popular figure amongst his people. I'm sure he owes much of his skill and guidance to you and I hope he appreciates that. But tell me Delia, why are your paintings signed Delia Wamalwa and not Delia Okomo?'

The time had come for Delia to break the news of her relationship with Winstone and explain why she had to keep it a secret from her family. The headmaster listened intently.

'Well,' he said at the end of her story, 'I would never have guessed it!'

'You were never meant to!' she said ruefully. 'Anyway, my pupils will continue to know me as Mrs. Okomo. It would take a great deal of explanation if I reverted to my real name. I really would like to remain at the school for two or three more years. I have some very promising pupils, and I would like to see them through their education. Then my wish would be to retire to take up painting full time.'

'So, let me get it straight then, there was no rich American supporting Winstone. It was you all along! Then why did I have to send him home through lack of fees?'

'The answer is simple: we hadn't realised we were mother and son at that time. He was only three when I had to leave him. You will appreciate he looks rather different now from a three-year old, and of course, I've aged over the years. He had always been told his mother had died. It was only as he was being sent home, he told me his background. Then I had my suspicions and he proved them right by bringing me my old yellow headscarf from home as a present on his return. If he hadn't had the foresight to do that, he might have gone through all his school years, and indeed we could have gone through the rest of our lives without knowing we were mother and son.'

Before he left, the headmaster came back to Delia. 'I've bought that portrait of Lenana for the school,' he said. 'We'll hang it near the entrance. Sipaya says he's delighted. It will also be a permanent reminder for us of one of our head boys and for you a recognition of your son's artistic ability.'

It was late by the time everybody had left. Mr. Kagwe came up to the four of them with a broad smile on his face and shook hands.

'This is one of the most successful previews I've held since I opened the gallery. Just look at the red dots everywhere. It's quite remarkable. It proves I know my clients, young man,' addressing Winstone, 'and that I know a good picture when I see one. Incidentally I invited a reporter from the Daily Nation to attend this evening's event, and I wouldn't be surprised if your name as a painter isn't established by tomorrow morning!'

When Winstone came to collect the unsold pictures at the end of the exhibition there were only five left, one of his mother's and four of his own. During the exhibition Mr. Kagwe had been given a letter addressed to Winstone which he handed to him. It was signed by Lydia Wakhungu. It turned out she was the girl who was late for school after watching him do the initial sketch of Mount Elgon. Lydia had also won a place at a national school in the capital. She had seen his picture with the painting in the newspaper and wondered whether it had been sold. Winstone wrote a reply saying the picture was given to a close friend of his and invited her to come to see it when she was next at home. Little did he know then that one day Lydia would become his wife.

As Winstone left with the remaining pictures Mr. Kagwe shook hands. 'I'll send you a cheque shortly.

You'll need to open a bank account if you haven't one already. I understand you'll be starting university this coming year. I reckon you've earned enough from the sale of your paintings to cover all your university fees and living expenses as well. Congratulations! I look forward to us developing a good working relationship in the future, you and I.'

CHAPTER TWENTY

A few weeks after Winstone's exhibition a well-spoken elderly gentleman called to see Mr. Kagwe. He introduced himself as Mr. Masinde.

'I'm sorry to trouble you,' he began. 'Somebody has drawn my attention to a newspaper cutting regarding an exhibition of paintings by a Mrs. D. Wamalwa and her son Winstone Wamalwa. My sister had a daughter who married a Wamalwa and had a son. She became a widow and then completely disappeared. From that time on we've found no trace of her. My sister who lives near Bungoma, is wondering whether the Mrs. Wamalwa who exhibited in your gallery is her missing daughter.'

Mr. Kagwe was intrigued. 'I have little knowledge of Mrs. Wamalwa. Indeed, I didn't know her name was Wamalwa until I saw the signature on her pictures. She often comes to my gallery to look at the paintings on exhibit. Painting is her particular interest. She's an art teacher at one of our national schools in the city, that I do know. I've no means of contacting her directly. Indeed, I doubt whether she has a telephone. Her son attended the same school and it's him I've spoken to largely in connection with his exhibition. I would be happy to give you the telephone number of the school if you would like, but of course it is the Christmas holidays at the moment and the school will not reopen again until early January.'

The gentleman thanked Mr. Kagwe for his help, took the telephone number with him and went on his way.

A day or two after the new term had started the secretary took a call from Mr. Masinde.

'I'm ringing about a family matter.' he said. 'An exhibition of paintings was held in the city some weeks ago. Two artists were involved. One of them was a Mrs. Wamalwa. My sister had a daughter who married a Wamalwa. Her husband died and after that his wife completely disappeared. That was a good number of years ago now. The gallery owner informed me that you have an art teacher at your school named Mrs. Wamalwa and my sister who lives near Bungoma is wondering whether your Mrs. Wamalwa is her missing daughter.'

'I'm sorry sir,' replied the secretary, 'but we have no-one of that name on our teaching staff.'

'But you have an art teacher, don't you?'

'Yes, we certainly do but her name is Mrs. Okomo. She's been with us for several years now.'

'Well, that's strange.' said Mr. Masinde. 'I do hope I have the correct telephone number. It's the number the gallery owner gave me. The other artist was supposed to be her son by the name of Winstone Wamalwa.'

'Winstone Wamalwa, yes. He was a pupil here.'

'I wonder then whether I could come to the school and meet him. He might be able to unravel this mystery.'

'I'm so sorry,' said the secretary, 'he was our head boy and a brilliant pupil at that, but he left us last term and will soon be on his way to university.'

'Oh dear! I do need to get to the bottom of this matter for the sake of my sister. Do you think it would be possible for me to make an appointment with the headmaster in case he can throw some light on this case?'

'I'll certainly ask him and if you let me have your telephone number, I'll ring you and let you know what he says.'

'It is a very odd matter isn't it,' the secretary said in the headmaster's office.

The headmaster sat and thought for a moment. It was only by chance he had learnt of Mrs. Okomo's predicament. He felt sorry for her. He realised the strain she must be under to keep her real identity a secret. The last thing he wanted to do was to reveal her proper name. He needed to put Mr. Masinde off the scent if he was to shield Delia.

'Tell him I'll be happy to see him, but I am unlikely to be able to give him much further information.'

Delia was called to see the headmaster in his office.

'A Mr. Masinde telephoned today to make an appointment with me next week.'

Delia's face dropped and paled. Before the headmaster could continue, she interrupted. 'Oh dear, that sounds like my uncle. That's bad news.'

'Yes, apparently he is. Somebody had drawn his attention to a newspaper article about the exhibition by a mother and son which named you as Mrs. Wamalwa and he's wondering whether you're his sister's missing daughter. I can see this is a serious situation for you, but I believe I can handle this matter. There's a conference in Thika next week about our controversial 8-4-4 education system. I'm sending you to it as a delegate so that you'll be out of the way when Mr. Masinde calls. If he asks to see you, I can then genuinely say you're away at a conference. My secretary told him when he rang that we have nobody on the staff with the name of

Wamalwa, but I decided to see him to put him off the scent, as it were. He had also asked to meet Winstone but of course he was informed he had left school in preparation for university. When he arrives, I'll simply confirm that our art teacher is Mrs. Okomo and has been on the staff for a several years. Since you told me your two families do not communicate with each other, I thought it might be a good idea if he went to speak to your father-in-law since from what you say he seems convinced you've died. If you're sure Winstone and his friend will have said nothing about your involvement with the exhibition it might well convince your uncle that the article was inaccurate. How do you feel about that, Delia?'

'Frankly I think you're a genius! I'm so grateful to you. I didn't know about a newspaper article until Mr. Kagwe said he had invited a reporter along. I was concerned at the time but since nothing seemed to come of it, I dismissed it from my mind. I'm convinced Winstone and his friend Absalom will have kept their mouths shut. They know too well what would happen if they didn't. And in any case, they're both setting off to visit Sipaya at his home shortly so are unlikely to be around when my uncle calls. You can imagine how thankful I'll be when it's safe for me to return to Cheptais again and give up all this pretence.'

The headmaster met Mr. Masinde in his office a few days later.

'I went back to Mr. Kagwe, the gallery owner, and he assured me Mrs. Wamalwa was a teacher at your school and she was Winstone's mother,' he said.

'Our art teacher is a talented painter herself, but her name is Mrs. Okomo. She's also a very devoted teacher and Winstone Wamalwa was one of her star pupils.

Winstone had talent of his own before he came to our school, but it was she who turned him into a painter of real ability. I think he has a great future ahead of him. Unfortunately, I really don't know how I can help you further. Winstone comes from a very poor background and came to us as an orphan. His grandparents brought him up. They could not afford his school fees and sadly he had to leave school. Fortunately, an anonymous donor heard of his plight and paid for him until he had finished his four years here.'

'I wonder whether it would be possible to meet Mrs. Okomo, Headmaster? It's a Luo name I know, but her maiden name may give us a clue.'

'Well of course, I wouldn't know about her maiden name. Had she been here I'm sure she could've enlightened you but just at the moment she's away at a conference in Thika.'

'Oh dear. That's a pity. It might have provided me with just the information I'm looking for.'

'Perhaps your sister might consider contacting Winstone's grandparents to see whether the missing lady has been in touch with them?'

'Sadly no,' said Mr. Masinde. 'The two families have never seen eye to eye with each other and there's been no contact between them.'

'May I suggest then that perhaps you might independently intercede with Winstone's grandparents to see if they've had any contact with their missing daughter-in-law? You'll surely know where they live.'

'Yes, indeed. I can verify their whereabouts from my sister.'

Mr. Masinde got up from his chair, shook hands and said, 'That's a helpful suggestion, Headmaster. I think it's the only way forward. I'm grateful for your time sir,' and made his way out of the office.

Elias was relaxing on the bench outside the house some days later when Mr. Masinde approached up the farm track. Elias got up to greet the stranger.

'I believe you are Mr. Elias Wamalwa?'

They shook hands.

'I'm sorry to disturb you. I've come on some family business. My name is Masinde, Jumo Masinde, and I'm an uncle of Delia Wamalwa.'

Elias was disturbed but he hid his feelings and said with a smile, 'I'm pleased to meet you. Come and sit down. I was just having a rest before I go back on the land. How can I help?'

'Well, it's a difficult matter. I've come here without my sister, Delia's mother, knowing. There was an exhibition of paintings in a gallery in Nairobi in November. I didn't see the exhibition myself. Somebody contacted me to say two artists were involved. One was Winstone Wamalwa, who I believe is your grandson, and the other was somebody named Delia Wamalwa. My sister wondered if that was her missing daughter.'

Elias was now very disturbed. 'I think that is extremely unlikely. We're pretty sure Delia has died. We've had no contact with her from the day she left here. She left in the middle of the night without any warning, leaving us to deal with an extremely disturbed grandson. You know, his father died only a week before. The loss of two parents in such a short time was more than any child could bear.'

'But did you know about the exhibition?'

'Yes of course. Winstone has a friend who shared his house here. He was invited up to join Winstone at the exhibition.'

'The gallery owner said that Mrs. Wamalwa was Winstone's mother and that she was his art teacher.'

'Well that can't be right,' said Elias. 'Mrs. Okomo was Winstone's art teacher. I know that because my eldest son and I visited him at school.'

'But did you actually meet Mrs. Okomo?'

'No, we didn't. We visited on a Saturday and she wasn't teaching then.'

'There's something mysterious about this whole thing and I can't get to the bottom of it,' said Mr. Masinde, throwing his hands on his knees in despair. 'How can it be that Mr. Kagwe said a Delia Wamalwa was Winstone's mother and art teacher and you and the school's headmaster, whom I have met, maintain that a Mrs. Okomo was his teacher? It doesn't make sense unless, of course, she remarried.'

'I agree,' said Elias, 'but I can't think she would have remarried without us knowing. Winstone would have been sure to tell us. You know, he was sent home during his third term at school because sadly, we were unable to pay for all his school fees. If his mother was alive and had remarried and was teaching at his school, I don't think that would have happened. She would surely have made up what was owing to the school. The only thing I can think is that this Mr. Kagwe has assumed the teacher was his mother and called her Mrs. Wamalwa in error and informed the newspaper accordingly.'

'There's one way to resolve this dilemma and that is to speak to Winstone himself. Is he around?'

'Well no, I'm afraid not. Winstone has gone off to stay with some Maasai friends somewhere near Narok. The boy was at school with him. And you know those people, they move around all over the place. You never know where they're going to be.'

'What about the friend who went up to Nairobi to be with him at the exhibition? He must know something. Can we speak with him?'

'Oh dear, no. You see the two of them have gone to visit the Maasai together.'

'Then I'm done for. It seems I'm not going to resolve this matter however much I try.' He shook his shoulders in resignation. 'It seems to me my sister is not going to get the closure she was hoping for.'

'As I said, we're convinced Delia has died but I can understand it won't help your sister until she has proof and that's something we would like to have as well, but sadly can't provide for her. I wish we could.'

Mr. Masinde stood up and shook hands. 'Well,' he said, 'I'm very grateful for your time. It's been pleasant talking to you.'

After Mr. Masinde had left Martha stepped outside. 'Who was that you were talking to?' she inquired. 'You talked to him for a long time. I didn't recognise him.'

'Believe it or not that was Delia's uncle!'

'Delia's uncle? Whatever did he want? I don't think we've met him before, have we?'

'Well, I don't remember him. He's a cultured well-spoken and well-dressed man quite unlike the rest of that family. It seems he might come from a professional background. You know that exhibition Winstone had in Nairobi? Well, he said there was a newspaper article which claimed it was a mother-and-son exhibition and named a Mrs. Wamalwa as the mother. I've never heard such nonsense in all my life! He said this Mrs. Wamalwa was also Winstone's art teacher at school. Well, that's rubbish too. We all know Mrs. Okomo is his teacher. I saw one of her paintings on the classroom wall. It was a beauty. I would love you to have seen it.'

'You don't think Delia remarried a Mr. Okomo, do you?' asked Martha.

'No, I don't. Winstone wouldn't have been sent home when we couldn't pay his fees. As one of her best pupils, and if Mrs. Okomo was his mother, she would surely have stepped in and paid up. John told me teachers in those schools are well paid.'

'Yes, but what about that anonymous donor?' Martha looked worried.

'If this Mrs. Okomo had paid, the school would have known about it. Besides, in his letter to me the headmaster indicated it was probably one of the school's ex-pupils from America who came to Winstone's rescue.'

'So why did he come here then?' asked Martha.

'He came on behalf of his sister. They were suspicious. I think they thought we knew all about Delia and hadn't told them. When you consider how much money Winstone made from those paintings I wouldn't mind betting they were after some of it.'

'I wouldn't put it past them either,' observed Martha.

'Anyway, I told him we had not heard from Delia since the time she left us and that we believed she was dead. I gather Mrs. Okomo also had one or two pictures of her own in the exhibition - at least that's what Winstone said. I told Mr. Masinde that the newspaper had probably got their facts muddled up and had assumed Mrs. Okomo was Winstone's mother. He was such a nice chap. So polite. I was sorry to disappoint him. He looked so downhearted when he left. I felt really sorry for him.'

'What do we do now?' asked Martha.

'We forget all about it. There's nothing more to be said,' Elias replied with conviction.

CHAPTER TWENTY-ONE

This is not quite the end of my story. Some four years later, after I finished at university, I returned home. My grandfather was then an old man. He was standing in his doorway when our smart white car turned into the farm track and stopped some distance from the house. We paused for a few moments, remembering things from the past then, being the driver, I was the first to get out of the car, followed by my passenger. Grandfather's sight was failing. He shielded his eyes from the sun with his hand and peered at us. I heard him call out to my grandmother.

'Martha,' he called, 'there's some visitors arrived.'

My grandmother joined him at the doorway.

'I can't make out who they are,' he was saying. 'That one, that man, looks a bit like Winstone.'

My grandmother followed his gaze.

'He walks like Winstone. Yes, I believe it's Winstone. Look at that smartly dressed woman he's with. She seems middle-aged.' I heard her say. 'What's he doing with a middle-aged woman? It isn't right you know, a boy of his age. It ought to be a woman much younger.'

I smiled to myself, hearing her comment. I walked slowly up the track, slightly ahead of my passenger. When we reached the house, I greeted my grandparents.

'*Mulembe* Grandfather, *mulembe* Grandmother,' and shook hands.

The lady stood a little behind me. My grandparents were curious. They were staring at the woman. There was not a flicker of recognition from either of them. I stepped back a pace or two, put my arm round the lady's waist and drew her forward.

'Grandfather, Grandmother,' I said, do you know who this is? Don't you recognise her? This is Delia, my beloved mother, the daughter-in-law you were always so fond of, the one you told me was dead. She was my art teacher at school, to whom I owe so much. She's come back home now, to be with you, to look after you, and to care for you in your old age.

BV - #0010 - 200123 - C0 - 203/133/14 - PB - 9781914424687 - Matt Lamination